SON of the SEA

Richard Pickard

Chicken House

2 PALMER STREET FROME
SOMERSET BA11 1DS

First published in Great Britain in 2023
Chicken House
2 Palmer Street
Frome, Somerset BA11 1DS
United Kingdom
www.chickenhousebooks.com

Chicken House/Scholastic Ireland, 89E Lagan Road, Dublin Industrial Estate,
Glasnevin, Dublin D11 HP5F, Republic of Ireland

Cover and interior design by Steve Wells
Cover illustration by Maxine Lee-Mackie
Typeset by Dorchester Typesetting Group Ltd
Printed and bound in Great Britain by CPI Group (UK) Ltd, Croydon CR0 4YY

FSC
www.fsc.org

MIX
Paper | Supporting
responsible forestry
FSC® C171272

1 3 5 7 9 10 8 6 4 2

British Library Cataloguing in Publication data available.

PB ISBN 978-1-913696-72-6
eISBN 978-1-915026-55-2

For Granny Pat, who loved her beach hut,
and Granny Norma who loved the sea.

ALSO BY RICHARD PICKARD

The Peculiar Tale of the Tentacle Boy

CHAPTER ONE

Banned

Casper scrutinized the water, his eyes straining to see past the light cloud of condensation which had settled on the inside of his swimming goggles.

Forty-nine more flutter kicks and then I'll switch to rotators, he thought, his large feet working up a small tsunami behind him as the water splashed all around. His arms were stretched out in front while his long legs did the hard work.

Forty-four, forty-three, forty-two.

Casper had been submerged for more than three hours, though he didn't plan on drying off any time soon. Not until he heard the familiar sound of Mrs Marsh's clapped-out car reversing into the driveway.

Thirty-seven, thirty-six.

Suddenly, Casper felt a small patch of pressure on the back of his head. He released a lungful of bubbles in surprise, and lifted his face from the water. A large frog, which had only just landed among his shaggy hair, leapt down on to his left hand – which clung to the bank of the pond.

'Thanks very much,' he said. 'You've made me lose count.'

Casper sat up, allowing himself to rest a little early. He lifted his goggles and popped them on to his forehead with a small *thwack* of the elastic. His knees sank down into the sludge, which lined the small pond and its bin-bag-padded bottom. They rolled in the mush with a satisfying squelch.

The garden seemed quieter than normal this morning.

A few dragonflies buzzed about the reeds that grew in long stalks by Casper's feet, but the newts which made their home in Mrs Marsh's ornamental pond were nowhere to be seen. Casper had once counted twenty-seven snails on the bottom, but even their numbers had dwindled. The water was certainly more murky than last Thursday, during his afternoon of dolphin kicks . . .

He felt something tickle his shoulder and flicked the pond skater crawling up his skin into the water with a deep breath.

'Better get back to it,' he said, snapping the goggles down over his eyeballs. 'Who knows how long it will be before—'

Casper stopped short, the thought silenced by the sound of a car door slamming shut. It had come from the other side of the large house which stood between the road and his makeshift swimming pool.

He leapt from the water, showering the neat lawn in dirty sploshes while he sprinted for the garden fence in great long strides. Once he reached it, Casper threw himself face first across the wooden trellis and landed in a knotted heap in the next neighbour's pristine yard.

'CASPER DELMARE, I *SEE* YOU!'

The disembodied but furious voice of Mrs Marsh

sailed over the fence. Casper could hear her shuffling frantically, tearing through the bramble bushes on her way to the edge of her property.

'I'm calling your parents this instant!' she yelled, snagging her dress on the spiky thorns which she'd planted as a Casper-deterrent. 'Do you know how long it's taken me to get the pH balance of my pond back to normal?'

Casper continued to run, leaping across the neighbouring garden's plastic neon furniture like Olympic hurdles. He made his way towards the green hedge, almost face-planting into its branches after catching an ankle on the outstretched claw of the pink flamingo fixed in the shrubbery. Righting himself, he forced his way through the sharp twigs and thorny leaves.

Just in time.

Mrs Marsh's reddened face peered furiously over the slatted wood of her own fence. 'Don't think I didn't see you, Casper Delmare! You'll pay for this, you rotten little delinquent! You *hooligan*!'

Casper had made it to the safety of his own concrete garden – a courtyard of grey nothingness – collapsing on to his back with a laugh. Adrenaline coursed through his body, closely followed by a rush of relief.

But . . . Mrs Marsh had said she'd be phoning his parents.

Casper sprang up and bolted towards the house, where he grabbed hold of the black drainpipe with both hands. Using his large but nimble feet, he quickly pushed his body up the brick wall and reached the open window of his bedroom. He hurled himself through and on to the carpet with a crash.

In the same moment, the downstairs telephone burst into life with a shrill ring that vibrated through the floorboards. Casper sat still, too scared to move a muscle in case he made even the slightest bit more noise until—

'CASPER!' his mother yelled up the stairs.

'Yes, Mum?' he called innocently, jumping on to the bed. He threw the thick duvet over his soaking wet body, just as his mother burst through the bedroom door.

'Don't "Yes Mum" me. You've been swimming in Mrs Marsh's garden pond again! She says you've swirled up all the silt, *and* caused her newts to relocate to the bird bath at number 23. She's at her wit's end!'

'Mum, I've no idea what she's talking about,' said Casper, his eyes wide. 'I've been in bed all morning.'

'Then why is your hair soaking wet?' his father asked, appearing in the hallway. 'And *why* are you wearing swimming goggles?'

'Oh.'

'Come downstairs,' said Mum. 'We need to talk.'

For as long as he could remember, Casper had been banned from swimming. The problem with this was that swimming was pretty much the only thing he cared about. His love of the water was so immense that he found himself unable to resist the urge to dive into a pond at every possible occasion! It didn't matter how much it embarrassed or annoyed his bossy parents ...

They both waited in the kitchen, their arms folded and with matching frowns.

'We've told you a thousand times,' his mother sighed. 'It isn't safe for you to go in the water.'

'But I have to swim,' Casper groaned in frustration, stomping green pond scum across the tiled floor. 'The water is in my blood. Swimming is what I was *born* to do!'

'You were *born* to make our lives an anxious mess,'

grumbled his dad, Roger. He stole a glance at his wife, Sophie, whose own expression had similarly thawed from anger into quiet unease.

'We'll keep you inside for the whole summer holiday if that's what it takes,' Mum promised. 'The last thing we want is to give the neighbours another reason to talk. I can almost hear them muttering as we speak . . .' She ran to the window and peeled back the lace curtain, squinting into the sunlit street.

'But I'm always careful,' protested Casper. 'No one knows anything except that I really like a swim. Even Mrs Marsh has never seen my feet!'

It was Casper's feet that made him certain swimming had been coded in his DNA from birth. He had been born with the most enormous pair of flippers! A fantastic set of webbed toes that helped to propel him through the water with the greatest of ease, rocketing Casper between the weeds and rubbish of ponds and fountains like a salmon swimming up a very dirty stream. But it was Casper's feet, too, that proved to be his biggest obstacle.

His parents were determined to keep them a secret.

'You've been lucky so far,' his father started. 'But

you can bet the neighbours will know something's up when you smell like a pond until it finally rains on Thursday. We've already checked the forecast.'

'There's not the slightest sprinkle for the next five days,' groaned Mum. 'I've had to cancel my badminton match again, since the sports centre showers are out of order.'

Swimming wasn't the only thing banned in the Delmare house. The building had been water-free for almost three years, forcing the family to shower in the back garden whenever it happened to rain. As for their thirst, Casper's mum would pummel every fruit or vegetable she found through an enormous juicer in an attempt to stave off dehydration. On a good day that meant a glass of orange juice, but as the weekly shop drew nearer Casper would have to pinch his nose and guzzle down a glass of pureed aubergine.

'I wouldn't have to jump in ponds and smell like a duck for days on end if you'd just let me swim,' continued Casper. 'I hate hiding who I am, but I do it for *you*!'

He had raised his voice – forcing his dad to press a finger to his lips and eye the kitchen wall which was shared by the neighbours.

'Please,' said Mum. 'You need to be more careful.'

Casper lifted his chin. 'I love my feet.'

'We know!' said Dad. 'But the world isn't so accepting, Casper. We can't just let those titanic toes flap about in the breeze like a string of sausages.'

'Webbed feet aren't so uncommon,' he insisted, heading over to the fridge. 'Frogs and ducks have them, don't they?'

'But people don't,' his father countered. The sound of Roger's heavy shoes slammed on the kitchen tiles as he paced back and forth. Casper pulled open the fridge door. 'People dislike large feet at the best of times, but your gargantuan paddles? You'd be a laughing stock! You'd end up in a laboratory, or at some grubby seaside aquarium. Have you seen what those places charge per visit?'

Casper rolled his eyes, his face hidden from his parents within the fridge. 'It's not as if I'm asking you to dig a swimming pool, or take me on holiday to Spain. The only time that I've ever even *seen* the sea is in my sleep! You've never let me go near it.'

Casper often visited the ocean in his dreams, when the longing to dive into its deepest blue would cause his heart to pound so hard that he'd wake up with a start.

He continued to rummage through the fridge, searching for something to drink among the stacks of Tupperware containers that each contained a different gloopy liquid. Even bottled water was banned after Casper had poured a litre of Highland Spring on the floor, and attempted to breaststroke the length of the kitchen.

'Of course we haven't let you near the sea!' laughed Mum. 'Why do you think we chose to move to Bramble-in-the-Oaks in the first place?' She paused, tapping her foot impatiently while she waited for Casper's full attention. 'There's a jug of pressed potato juice on the bottom shelf!'

His parents had barely made it past Casper's first birthday before they'd stuck a drawing pin in a map of Great Britain and found themselves the furthest town from the coast in the whole country! *Bramble-in-the-Oaks*. A barren smudge without so much as a river in sight, forcing Casper to get his watery fix from the neighbour's pond instead.

'Where did we live before?' asked Casper, grabbing the container and pouring himself a glass of cloudy, beige liquid. His parents blushed and their eyes quickly found each other, widening as they did each time this topic arose. Casper knew that the question was forbidden, but he was sick of never getting answers.

'Casper, that's enough,' his dad snapped, marching loudly from the room. 'Consider yourself grounded for the rest of the week!'

'What?!'

His mother followed closely, leaving behind a haze of citrus perfume from the dry lemon peel that she'd rubbed on her neck that morning.

Alone, Casper took a sip from his glass of milky potato juice and shuddered at the starchy taste. He sighed, rippling his toes in the small puddle of murky pond water which had pooled on the floor around his flabby webbed feet.

CHAPTER TWO

The News Report

The weather forecast was wrong, as usual. By Friday it still hadn't rained, which meant that a green-tinged Casper had spent the final days of term sitting at his school desk and stinking of Mrs Marsh's pond.

He *hated* living in Bramble-in-the-Oaks.

But now, it was summer!

Six glorious weeks of freedom lay ahead, and

Casper had planned the entire holiday in his mind – taking note of his parents' schedules so that he could sneak out and swim in every pond or puddle he could find in his desolate town.

After the final school bell rang, Casper made his way home and dutifully marched upstairs to his bedroom – even though he thought it was pretty rubbish of his parents to ground him again. *Why was being proud of his marvellous toes such a big deal?*

Kicking off his cumbersome shoes, Casper slumped to the floor of his bedroom and stripped the socks from his feet. He fanned them in blissful relief.

Much better, he thought. *Just one more day and I'll be free to find some water!*

Wanting a pick-me-up, Casper crawled across the room towards his wardrobe, where he yanked a drawer open and rummaged through a fluffy pile of pants. Finally, he pulled out a battered videotape – its white label curling back at the corners. His spirits quietly lifted, Casper rolled over to the tiny television in the corner and shoved the tape inside with the sole of his foot. As the clunky contraption crackled into life, he grabbed a half-drunk glass of cauliflower juice from the bedside table and sank into a ball on the floor.

He watched intently.

A shimmering blue filled the wobbly picture and a voice buzzed from behind the speakers, fizzling from the videotape's overuse.

'Beryl, what a swim!' cheered a news reporter as his face appeared on-screen. 'How does it feel to have achieved something at seventy-five that most of us could only *dream* of at half your age?' he asked. The reporter shoved a fuzzy microphone under the bony chin of a woman dressed in a latex swimming suit.

'It's all right really,' buzzed Beryl the Bazooka, who had made the national news after becoming the oldest person to ever swim across the English Channel. 'I knew I could do it, or I wouldn't have gone to all that effort, would I?' Her long fingers reached up to a rubbery, flowery swimming cap on her head. She pulled it off with a pop to reveal a bright shock of short pink hair, until the top bounced back into its mohawk like a spiky fluorescent spine.

'What would you say to any fans of the Bazooka, watching this at home and wondering whether they could replicate your achievement for themselves?'

'There's not many people out there who want to be bothering with all that training. You've got to truly love it. You've got to feel the ocean running through your soul if you've any hope of being up at dawn and into the freezing cold water before the milkman has woken up.'

Beryl looked directly into the camera while Casper mouthed along to the long-memorized interview, feeling the familiar sensation that she was talking directly to him:

'For some people, the sea is in their blood. If you wake up in the morning and all you can think about is swimmin', then maybe you might have what it takes to swim the English Channel an' all.'

Casper had recorded the news report one balmy August evening a few years earlier. Locked in his room for leaping inside the neighbour's water storage tank, he'd turned on the television and learnt of Beryl's record-breaking achievement. She quickly became his hero, and after watching the footage almost every day since, the seed of an idea had been planted in Casper's mind.

The idea that, one day, he might swim the English Channel too . . .

And be the *youngest* person to ever do it.

After fishing the following day's newspaper from

the bin, Casper had plastered Beryl the Bazooka's story across the back of his wardrobe and a mini shrine took shape – hidden behind the hanging clothes and piles of heavy, clumpy shoes. Soon the news clippings were joined by postcards, drawings and maps which he sellotaped alongside, covering the walls like a museum of ambition. In a battered old atlas, Casper traced Beryl's zigzag swimming route from a small town called Corallium, which jutted from the south coast like a thumb, across the water to the northern shore of France.

The words from her television interview echoed through his head in every waking moment: 'You've got to have faith in your dream, because no one else is gonna hand it to you. It's up to you to reach out for it, grab it tight an' make sure it comes true.'

Casper sighed deeply.

He rewound the videotape and pressed play for the fourth time in a row. Swimming the Channel had become an obsession for him almost overnight, but time was running out.

By the autumn he'd be twelve . . .

Too old to set his own record as the youngest person to ever swim it.

A crack of thunder suddenly drew his attention from the television. He paused the video on Beryl's beaming face and ran to the window. The heat of summer had finally risen to a crescendo in the clouds overhead, where the evening sky was tearing open like an old wound.

'At last!' Casper cheered, watching as large bullet-like droplets of rain began to hammer on the window and the concrete garden behind. He tore off his smelly school uniform and ran through the house in his undies, both his skin and his stomach screaming with thirst.

Throwing the back door open he leapt outside into the rain, spinning on the spot, his arms stretched wide while the cool water pummelled his body like the best power shower in the world. Casper lay on his back and allowed the rain to wash over him, imagining that he was far away from Bramble-in-the-Oaks and everyone who didn't understand him . . .

He was adrift at sea, the waves of the English Channel rolling across his chest with a cool sting. Sea foam slapped at the nape of his neck, and everything was right with the world, if only for a moment, and if only in his mind.

CHAPTER THREE

Gouda

'Mum, Dad, *please* let me come. I promise I'll behave. I'll only jump in the fountain once you're inside the supermarket and no one can tell we're related.'

It was Saturday morning and the weekly shop was well overdue. The previous night's dinner had been leftover leftovers, and Casper had been sent to bed with a glass of stale cabbage juice.

'You must be joking,' his mother laughed. 'We'll be watching your ankles disappear through the sunroof and out of sight the second the car stops.'

'Please!' Casper fell to his knees and clung to his mother's waist. 'I'll just have a quick paddle in the water, I swear. No one will see my feet.'

'Absolutely out of the question!' came a bark from the kitchen, where Casper's dad was doing a final check of the freezer. 'You and those colossal hooves have seen the water for the very last time. It's for your own good, son.'

'Hooves?' frowned Casper. He shook his head. 'I need to practise every chance that I have if I'm going to swim the English Channel and be just like Beryl the Bazooka.'

'Beryl the Bazoo—' his father gasped, his left eye twitching wildly while a bead of sweat formed on his forehead. 'Have you been watching that blooming tape again? Listen to me, Casper. You aren't going anywhere near the sea, let alone swimming the flipping Channel. The last thing we want is to see you carted off to SeaWorld, performing three shows a day. There's a reason we make you wear wellies when you shower in the rain, you know. We want you to be safe, don't you understand?'

Casper collapsed into a pile by the door.

'Swimming the Channel,' sighed Mum. 'Honestly, Casper. Imagine the publicity if you actually made it to France? We'd never be able to keep your feet a secret, and we didn't move to the middle of nowhere for nothing.'

Her words floated gently down each of Casper's ear canals, forcing his dream from the previous night to pop back into his brain like an old projector whirring to life. He had been sitting in the surf, splashing the water at the edge of an endless blue sea. The shallow waves had felt cool as they crashed against his feet, the webbed skin between his baby toes barely visible.

It had all seemed so real to Casper, just as the recurring dream did on each and every occasion it woke him in the early hours of the morning. But it couldn't be anything more than his overactive imagination. Despite the urgent longing that he felt for the sea, Casper had never even *seen* it.

Unless . . .

'*Where* did we live before?' he asked, flinching as the nagging question left his lips.

'Enough,' said his mother. 'Just please, stay here and . . . stay dry. For me?'

His parents disappeared through the front door with a bang.

Casper groaned. The thought of being kept from the water was unbearable. It had been so hot lately that he'd secretly been holding his webbed feet against the cool chrome of the barren kitchen's waterless taps.

But he had a plan.

Not in a million years had he really thought his parents would bring him on a jaunt to the supermarket fountains without a fight. Reaching into the pocket of his shorts, he pulled out his mother's car key which he'd grabbed from her handbag when he'd flung his arms around her waist. He dove through the back door and out into the garden.

Moments later, he heard his parents re-emerge through the front door.

'Honestly, can't you tell the difference between car keys and shed keys?' grumbled Roger, his shirt growing damper by the second.

'Well, these were in the drawer where my car ones are kept. Why would the shed keys be left in the hallway? Tell me that!'

The couple continued to bicker as they combed the hallway in a frustrated search. Meanwhile, Casper slipped over the fence at the side of the house and silently crept towards their car. He popped open the boot and jumped inside between the empty bags and oil cans, tossed the key to the ground and let the lid quietly close above him. In the same moment, his parents left the house once again – growing wearier by the second.

'. . . the key is kept in *that* drawer. Perhaps you've left the car one by the garden shed. Wait, look!' spluttered Sophie, bending down to pick up the actual keys which were now abandoned on the gravel driveway. 'It's here, I told you I had them. You must have dropped them.'

'I didn't drop anything,' Roger said through gritted teeth. 'Let's just go.'

Which they did, all the while oblivious to the boy hiding in their boot.

For the next fifteen minutes Casper held on tightly, bashing his head with every bump of the road, until finally he felt the car slowly roll to a stop. He listened intently, nervously waiting until the moment that the lock popped open and then . . . he sprang forth like a tropical bullfrog, diving between his father's outstretched arms and the pile of empty shopping bags which he'd come to collect.

'Boy, get back here *now*!' screamed Roger, as Casper's discarded clothes blew towards him through the wind left by his son. 'Don't you even *think* about it!'

But it was too late.

Casper was half-dressed, kicking his feet free of the enormous, square-toed shoes that his mother forced him to wear, while he made a barefoot sprint for the supermarket fountains – his favourite swimming pool in the entire world.

Well, the biggest sort-of pool he'd ever managed to swim in, anyway.

Meanwhile his furious father jumped back inside the car, ready to drive away in a sooty cloud of exhaust and exhaustion. Sophie placed a quivering hand on the steering wheel.

'We need *food*,' she groaned, exasperated. Her stomach rumbled as if on cue. She looked towards the fountains, now occupied by their lanky son, who seemed to be warming up with a backstroke. 'No one has seen that he's with us. We'll steer a clear berth from the water and just let him get on with it. I'll be with you all the way.'

A glance passed between them and after a pause, the pair climbed from the car and moved slowly towards a long line of metal trolleys. They picked one as far from the fountains as they possibly could, leaving Casper to cheerfully guzzle grey water. He butterflied his way around the concrete basin and counted the silver change, free of the constraints of his clumpy shoes and feeling the happiest he'd felt in weeks.

Inside the supermarket, the familiar chaos of Saturday morning waited. An army's worth of mums and dads traversed the store like they were tackling a military assault course – diving between clashing trolleys filled with screaming toddlers and their piles of slowly melting frozen meals. On the dairy aisle, wedged beside an icy cabinet filled with imitation butter and an assortment of fromage frais, stood a shivering elderly saleswoman dressed in a Dutch bonnet, apron and an oversized pair of wooden clogs.

'*Goedemorgen*,' she croaked uncertainly, with a

Birmingham accent as thick as cement. 'Would you like to try some Gouda? We've a special on all week.'

She meekly proffered a plate of cubed cheese to passing punters, all while standing in front of an enormous wheel of Gouda which loomed above her like a red, waxy moon. Flinching at the clammy, grabbing hands of passing children, the saleswoman did her best to fade into the background.

Unfortunately for her, a young couple caught a whiff of the cheesy goodness on offer and stopped to partake. Their one-year-old, sitting in the front of their trolley, reached out to the woman with a shriek of delight and visibly sticky red fingers. Recoiling in horror and with a sudden lurch, the saleswoman slipped from the heels of her wooden shoes and fell backwards into the display – bringing the couple with her. As the giant brown clogs soared dramatically through the air in slow motion, the entire stand came crashing down in a pile of bodies and broken cocktail sticks. The enormous Gouda was freed from its perch with such a force that it was sent careering across the supermarket like a Ferris wheel loose of its hinges.

Sadly for the Delmares, it was at that very moment that Roger and Sophie turned on to the chilled food aisle to be met face on by an angry wheel of waxed cheese . . .

A short while later Casper sat inside a sterile hospital room, staring at his parents who lay side by side in long, metallic beds. They were propped up on a mountain of crispy white pillows, their limbs hanging from the ceiling on thin metal wires and their heads wrapped in tight cotton bandages. Their jaws, which Casper knew would usually have been quick to cast the blame, were wired shut – forcing the pair to make do with muted, angry stares that seemed to burn his damp skin.

As much as Casper had hoped for a summer free of interference, he could never have imagined that his parents would be taken out by a wheel of cheese. It might have sounded a little funny on paper . . . but they were his only family! Even though they were strict, Casper knew deep down that it came from a place of love. He hated to see them injured.

Besides . . . where was he supposed to stay all summer with them out of action?

As if his thoughts had been picked up on a radio frequency, a police sergeant entered the room holding a large folder filled with paperwork.

'Casper, my name is Sergeant Kirtley,' she started solemnly, tearing a few tissues from a box and offering them in earnest. 'I know it's been an odd morning, but I've got some good news! We've managed to reach your grandmother, who has agreed that you must go and stay with her for the summer. Won't that be nice? It's just until your parents are fighting fit and able to look after you again.'

Casper wasn't sure that he had heard correctly. 'My . . . grandmother? I have a grandmother?'

The sergeant's smile dissolved in an instant, her face matching Casper for confusion. Her eyes darted between the frightened frowns of Roger and Sophie, who were each silently vibrating with worry from their beds.

'Yes, Casper, your father's mother, Ida,' she continued with unease. 'She lives in a lovely town called Corallium with her wife. I'm sure that you'll have a brilliant time there.'

Casper held her gaze but still showed no sign of recollection.

He looked at his parents, their wired jaws glinting in the brilliant white of the hospital lights. Their restless eyes scanned his face, waiting for the inevitable . . .

'Corallium!' cried Casper. The penny had dropped. 'Did you say my grandmother lives in Corallium? I've seen that town on the map inside my wardrobe. It's where Beryl the Bazooka began her Channel swim . . . It's on the sea!'

'Er, yes,' the sergeant stuttered with rapidly growing concern, while the Delmares practically frothed behind their bandages. 'But you didn't know that you had a grandmother?'

'Not exactly,' said Casper, a wide and wonderful smile spreading across his face. 'But I'm sure she'll be lovely!'

For his whole life, Casper had felt an unknowable longing to be beside the sea, and now, he was actually going to *see* it. Not in one of his recurring dreams, but in real life.

He was going to Corallium.

CHAPTER FOUR

To the Sea

$\mathcal{A}$rmed with a small suitcase, packed under the watchful gaze of the police sergeant, Casper had been bundled on to a stuffy coach and on to a summer by the sea.

After what seemed like hours of winding country lanes and tight corners, finally the coach came to a sudden halt beside a large village green. The driver looked over his shoulder and called down the aisle to

Casper: 'Son, this is your stop. Corallium Castle.'

Casper glanced around nervously, dripping wet after leaping into a canal during the short pitstop at a service station. Of course he'd packed his best pair of swimming trunks – a fraying ball of spandex made in secret after cutting up a pair of his mum's blue leggings.

At first glance, Corallium didn't look much like the seaside. There were no video arcades, or ice cream vendors. There were no *kids*!

And where, most importantly, was the sea?

'I'm sorry, but are you sure?' he asked, walking to the driver with his suitcase under one arm.

'Positive.'

'I was told we were coming to the seaside?'

The driver barked a booming laugh which echoed down the length of the near-empty coach. 'We're by the sea, all right; I can promise you that.' He took a deep breath and closed his eyes. 'Can't you feel that?'

'Feel what?' Casper asked, more confused than ever.

'The sea does something funny to people. At least to some people, including yours truly.' The driver's face was thoughtful.

'Funny how?' Casper felt a tingle of anticipation in his webbed toes.

'They're drawn to the seaside like a current. It's right here.' The driver rubbed his belly with a palm. 'A dull ache, in the pit of your stomach. Don't you know what I mean?'

Casper stood very still, mouth agape. He'd never met anyone else who'd understood that feeling.

'Um . . .'

'It's like somethin' wants you to stay here, for ever,' the driver continued. 'You can feel it too, can't you?'

The familiar niggle began to swell inside Casper, an urge which propelled him towards the water. It was like a hunger, which sank from his stomach right down to the very tips of his webbed toes.

'I can,' he replied at last. 'I always can.'

'Then you're in the right place!' The driver smiled, as though snapping back to reality. 'There are a million an' one stories about this place. Aquatic tales which go back for centuries. It doesn't get much more *seaside* than Corallium.'

Casper breathed a sigh of relief. So he *was* in the right place, and closer to the sea than ever. His toes shuddered with excitement.

'Thank you,' he offered the driver, hopping down on to the pavement beside a tiny roundabout marked with a tall stone needle. The coach driver sat at the wheel, his hands gripping its leather. It seemed to Casper as if the man were fighting an urge to leap from the vehicle and follow him, his teeth clenched in longing . . . But finally he sighed, and the doors snapped shut. The coach moved away from the kerb and away down the lane in a sad splutter of fumes.

Casper looked around at the strange town, which appeared to be a web of several long cobbled lanes – each one running out from the stone needle like beams of light. Looking at the ground, he saw that the cobbles weren't stone but in fact a mosaic-like pattern made up of what seemed to be the mould fossils of shells. Thousands of them lined the ground like the ghostly imprints of ancient seaside skeletons in every shape and size.

Odd, thought Casper.

How would so many shellfish, bound to the sea, have found their final resting place up here on dry land? The driver had said something about Corallium's aquatic tales.

Is this what he meant?

The sudden toot of a car horn made him spin on the spot. With a gasp of delight, Casper realized that he was standing in the shadow of a castle's craggy remains. A twisted lump of greyish pink, with tall spires rising high above the village like four fingers reaching up from a knotted fist. The castle had the strangest quality, as if it had been crafted from a coral reef. To Casper, it felt like the castle might have once been a living, breathing organism.

But that was ridiculous.

He looked around again, noticing the tall and mossy trees which ran along the streets in every direction. Their lengthy olive trunks rose up to burst into slick green stalks of wilted spinach that hung down over the pavements like long strands of hair. It was as if a great wave had receded, leaving the land littered with seaweed.

The sight of seagulls in the sky pulled Casper across the street and down one of the sloping pavements lined with shops. Here, the fossilized cobbles seemed to glow neon beneath the large letters of a *BINGO* sign which flashed a half-hearted red. Beside the bingo hall were a souvenir shop and a dusty hair salon, displaying an array of styles in the window and claiming to deliver the longest-lasting blue rinse in the county (whatever that was).

Casper's heart was momentarily buoyed by the sight of an old-fashioned sweet shop, but on closer inspection it seemed to only sell hard pebble-like mints. Next, inside a funny-smelling cafe that promised 'pre-mashed meals', Casper spied a woman struggling under the weight of an enormous bag filled with prunes. She tipped them into a metal contraption that gushed out a purple sludge.

'Casper?'

A voice made him jump in surprise.

He turned to see an elderly woman smiling at him. She was exceptionally tall, and might have looked familiar if his dad had ever managed to crack a smile himself. The woman wore a glossy navy trench coat that was tied at her waist with a belt. Its light fabric glistened in the sun like a lizard's scales, and Casper found himself resisting the urge to reach out and stroke it. Soft, dark hair curled around the back of the woman's ears, and at her feet was a fluffy wire fox terrier attached to a lead which fell from her hand. She rattled with the sound of chunky black bangles that clattered together at her wrists, the sheen of which matched a thick rope of black pearls resting on her collarbone.

'Casper, I'm your Granny Ida. And this is Triton,' she said, motioning to the small dog now sniffing Casper's shins in welcome. 'It's lovely to have you here. Though, of course, I wish it were under happier circumstances.'

'Could you take me to the sea?' Casper blurted, forgetting his manners in a haze of salt air which hovered over him like a red mist. He bent down and scratched the dog's ears. 'I'm sorry, I mean, hello, Granny Ida. It's really nice to meet you.'

'And you too, Casper,' smiled Ida, with only the slightest suggestion of offence.

'Thanks,' he paused. 'So, *would* you take me to the sea?'

Ida's face stiffened into a frown this time, a flicker of worry betraying her air of effortless warmth for an instant – but long enough for Casper to notice.

'I'm just excited,' he blushed.

'Well, never mind the sea right now. We need to get you home, and—' She looked at his clothes, still wet from the canal. 'Dry.'

*

Ida's house was a curious construction just a short walk from the castle. A strange mound of grey gabbro rock, the building's jagged shape made it seem as though it might have been carved from the cliff face on which it stood, or else pushed up through the waves by a great movement of the earth. Although it was four storeys tall, the house was barely the width of Casper's old concrete garden, which gave him the distinct impression it might topple over. He looked to the top floor and saw that several large windows were thrown wide open, allowing huge swathes of white fabric to billow freely in the wind. The sheets poured from the building like steam, stretching high above the roof like the sails of a gigantic ship which cut across the blue sky.

'Granny, what are those for?' he asked, flabbergasted.

'What's what for?' she replied, following the point of his finger with her eyes.

Casper looked back towards the house and saw that the sails had disappeared. The windows were closed tight, their polished glass reflecting the fluffy shapes of a few white clouds. It had been a long day . . .

'Never mind,' he said, batting the image from his thoughts.

Approaching the weathered front door, which was framed by a mosaic zigzag of pink and orange shells, Casper noticed a crooked wooden sign which pointed into an overgrown bush. He looked closer, seeing that a narrow pebble path in fact ran beside the house and down through the tall grass behind.

The sign read:

To the sea

Struggling against the pull of his desire, as Ida's dog Triton also tugged his lead in a similar direction, Casper found himself being ushered inside the dark house. The shells which adorned the threshold reflected a pearl-like shimmer on the tiled floor, before the door came to a heavy close.

Casper followed Ida up a seemingly endless staircase, passing several rooms on the way which included a lounge on the first landing beside a hallway cupboard, and a large bedroom on the second that Casper supposed must be Ida's.

'Is your wife here?' he asked.

'Wife?' said Ida, suddenly flustered. 'Oh, no. She . . . We . . . We were never actually married. I mean, it's just me now, I'm afraid. It has been for quite a while.'

'I'm sorry,' said Casper apologetically, cringing at his question and cursing the sergeant for her painfully out-of-date intel.

By the time they reached the third floor, he had noticed that almost every wall in the house was stained by rectangular patches of colour – the shadows of picture frames which had once hung in their place.

Weird, he thought, before the question was washed from his tongue as they arrived in the roof of the stone house. There, Casper found a cosy room had been hastily tidied and turned into what might resemble a child's bedroom. An assortment of second-hand books and some musty toys were laid out on a shelf, next to a bed dressed in crisp white sheets that were trimmed with stuffy lace.

'It's nothing much,' Ida beamed with apparent satisfaction. 'But it's a real pleasure to have you here. This house could do with a shot of youth, not to mention Corallium! Your arrival will have brought the average age down by forty years.'

Casper dropped his suitcase on the bed as his attention was drawn to a picture frame perched on the windowsill. A young man looked up to the camera from a red-and-yellow coral-patterned carpet.

His dad.

A baby Casper sat on his father's lap and smiled with a toothy grin. He must have been around one year old.

'I hope you'll have a lovely summer here, Casper,' said Ida joyfully. She perched on the edge of the bed, her legs stretched out as she placed one large and glossy shoe on top of the other. 'We don't know each other well yet, but I can tell that we'll get along famously!'

A thought floated into the forefront of Casper's mind.

'Why *don't* we know each other?' he asked broodingly, picking up the picture frame. 'You must have known about *me* if you had this, so why don't I know about *you*?' He peered down at the photo, but except for the coral carpet there were no other clues as to where it had been taken.

Ida was caught off guard, stammering slightly before she formed a response. 'Th-that's a funny story,' she said with an air of dismissal. 'I'm sure your parents can tell you another time, once they've recovered, of course.'

Casper placed the picture frame back down, ready

to push the subject further, but was distracted by the view from the window behind. It was the most perfect sight, which seemed to dance on his eyeballs like a hypnotic piece of music: the largest, most magnificent endless blue – more beautiful than he could have ever imagined it would be.

For the first time in his waking life, he looked out at the sea.

'Granny, can we *please* go down to the water now?' he blurted, pulling the window open. His webbed toes throbbed, threatening to burst through the leather of his shoes.

Ida's frown returned.

'The sea?' she huffed. 'It's an awful thing, really. Big and wet. Deeper than anything. Snakes in the heather, sand everywhere – stuck in places you've never...' She trailed off, looking out of the window.

Casper ignored her and rested his head in his hands, absorbed by the immaculate view. The water continued to shimmer far below, its blue surface broken only by a few tufts of white foam which copied the clouds overhead. A new thought occurred ... He leant his shoulders out of the window, twisting his neck towards the roof and half expecting to find that the billowing white sails of a sky ship were once again flying over the house.

But now, even the clouds had disappeared.

Casper turned back to Ida, who was still sitting frozen on the edge of his bed.

'Granny?' he asked, causing Ida to snap-to. Triton licked the tips of her fingers which had fallen with her arms to the side. Her thick bracelets smashed together as she regained her thoughts with a scratch of her head.

'What? The sea? No, no. Now is not the time for any of that. We need to make some tea, and I need to hear all about your journey down from Bramble-in-the-Oaks! I haven't ridden a coach in years, it must have been such a treat!' She coughed. 'Circumstances aside.'

Casper's stomach ached with longing as he stared at the wave pattern on his granny's teacup. The lines began to wobble like the real-life tide and his thoughts lingered on the sea, which felt painfully close by after so many years. After an hour of small talk, Granny Ida had fallen asleep – her head drooping forward while her heavy pearls swung delicately in time with her snores . . .

Could he slip down to the water? And *should* he? What would be his excuse?

Triton whimpered and batted the sitting room door with his nose. An idea popped into Casper's head like Corallium's bright *BINGO* sign flickering to life. He bolted from the sofa, abandoning his luke-warm tea, and hopped down the stairs to the hallway with Triton in his wake – a piece of shortbread clamped in his teeth. Casper quickly rummaged in the kitchen drawer and found the dog's lead, knocking an old set of keys to the floor as he pulled it from the depths. He picked them up and saw a mermaid keyring swinging from the chain. There were words written on her tail in black pen:

Beach Hut 702

'A beach hut!' he cheered. 'But it doesn't sound like Granny has a lot of love for the beach. Why would she bother having a beach hut?'

There was no time to wonder.

Casper had more pressing business. He *had* to get to the water, before Ida woke up. He pocketed the beach hut keys, attached the lead to Triton's collar and charged through the front door into the evening sun.

CHAPTER FIVE

Beach Hut 702

Casper walked down the pebble path behind Ida's house, the smell of damp pine needles and warm grass filling his nose. Triton tugged him furiously forward, his lead stretched tight.

'Calm down, boy,' he panted. 'It's like Granny hasn't brought you down here in for ever.'

Secretly he felt the same. Butterflies pummelled his insides, and his webbed toes throbbed as if they were deep in the ocean already.

The path led Casper through banks of grass even taller than him, which chirped and rustled with the sounds of crickets and other invisible insects before a canopy of sprawling trees briefly blotted out the sun. The squawks and hoots of birds in the bushes echoed through the empty woodland as a warm and salty breeze drew him onward.

When they finally came to the bottom of the path and swapped the cloak of trees for summer's evening light, the woodland opened on to a dazzling field of swaying purple heather. A sandy trail slipped through the middle like a thin yellow river. Casper followed the curve out from the small forest and a wooden sign, planted among the flowering undergrowth, caught his eye. He swallowed hard as he read it:

Caution – Adders

'Ida wasn't lying, then, Triton. There really are snakes!' He looked down into the scrubland uncertainly, scanning the heather for the slightest movement as Triton sniffed at the nearest stem. 'We better stick to the sand.'

They carried on and at last the path rose up

towards a row of grass-speckled sand dunes, the heather fading into a river of thirsty weeds, and every thought evaporated from Casper's brain when the horizon was finally revealed.

A glistening blue threatened to burst his head with exhilaration.

At last, giving in to the persistent tug of Triton's lead, Casper broke into a run. Cresting the steepest dune, a boulder split in two by the path and covered in tall grass which sprouted in huge clumps like matted hair, he found a golden field of pristine sand. Here, a smattering of elderly bathers were packing up their towels and windbreakers. Behind them, the sea was even better than in his recurring dreams and more brilliant than the view from Ida's home.

'I can't believe it!' he cried aloud.

Cresting waves broke into sea foam on the surface, tumbling down into the sandy shore like an avalanche of freshly powdered snow.

'Err,' came a sudden and surprising voice behind him. '*Who* are *you?*'

Casper turned to find a girl around his age standing beneath the dune. She was wearing an electric-blue wetsuit and carrying a large surfboard casually under one arm. Her dark, damp hair was slicked down her back in a tight fishtail braid which dripped on to the sand. She stood at the edge of a bumpy path of wooden planks which stretched behind her, decorating the seafront in a crooked zigzag that lined the front of the dunes and wound into the distance.

'I'm Casper, who are you?'

'I'm Wynn,' said the girl with a smile of shock and delight.

'That's a funny name,' he replied as he skidded down the sand dune towards her.

'Says *Casper*!' she huffed. 'I like my name. It means friend.'

'Hi, Wynn,' laughed Casper. 'I could use a few friends down here, I'm not sure I've seen anyone younger than seventy since I arrived.'

'Well, don't get too excited,' said Wynn, stabbing the end of her surfboard into the sand where it stood unsupported. 'You're the first kid my age I've ever seen in Corallium. I have to hang around with my older brother, Tan, when I'm not surfing. Even my *dad* is young for this place, and he's forty-five.'

The small bubble of hope in Casper's chest burst. 'Forty-five?'

'I know, right? He's an archaeologist. He moved us here so he could explore the "historical origins of Corallium". She rolled her eyes. 'As if anyone but him believes those stories.'

'What stories?' asked Casper.

'You don't know?' said Wynn, surprised. She adopted a deep and important voice: 'Legend says that Corallium was once a city beneath the sea and that the castle itself was built from the coral and sand of the seabed. You've seen the shell pavements, right?'

Casper nodded, his mind whirling with images of an ancient city populated by merfolk.

'My dad says the mould fossils are proof that Corallium's streets have existed for thousands of years, and that they once ran along the sea floor,' continued Wynn. 'He's digging up the castle grounds, looking for evidence. I'll be down here surfing every day now it's the holidays. There's not much else happening around here, except for bingo.'

'That's all right with me,' beamed Casper, turning back to the shimmering blue waves. 'All I need is the water.'

'Do you surf?' asked Wynn, enthusiasm radiating

from her in waves like the water still crashing behind them.

'No, I'm a swimmer,' Casper replied. He puffed out his chest with pride. It was the first time he'd ever said that out loud. It felt amazing.

'Well, you won't be alone. Everyone comes to Corallium to retire, but before long they're running marathons and long-distance swimming. I swear there's something in the water. Tan was a swimmer too, until . . .'

Triton barked as Wynn trailed off.

'And who's this?' she continued, apparently grateful for the distraction. She dropped to the ground and the dog began to clamber up her wetsuit. He licked her brown face with fervour. 'I've never seen you down here, either.'

'You haven't?' asked Casper, surprised. 'This is my granny's dog. She's Ida Delmare? I think she has a beach hut along here . . . I'm staying with her for the summer, in the really tall house at the top of the path.'

Wynn continued to scratch Triton's head while she looked up at Casper. 'That house is so weird,' she said. 'It makes you think the legends might be true, as if it was once the cave of a sea god or something. I always wondered who lived there. I've never met an Ida, though.'

Casper's mind continued to whirr. Why did Granny have a beach hut if she never came down to the seafront? And how could someone live so close to the water, but not feel that same pull to the ocean that he did?

The same pull that everyone who came through Corallium did!

'So, you're a swimmer,' said Wynn. 'Are you any good?'

'The best!' Casper glowed, the change of topic pushing everything else from his mind. 'Before I turn twelve, I'm going to break a record and become the youngest person to swim the English Channel.'

'Keep your voice down!' cried Wynn with alarm, reaching out to clamp her hand across Casper's mouth. 'That record is cursed!'

'What?' he said, his response muffled through Wynn's fingers. She released him, leaving a layer of scratchy dry sand on his lips. 'What do you mean, cursed?'

'No one has broken that record in sixty years, and every single kid that's tried has had some kind of . . .

Terrible! Accident!' She punctuated the words with great emphasis, waving her arms dramatically in the air.

Casper stared at her, unfazed. 'You *are* joking, right?'

'Actually, no,' replied Wynn earnestly. 'Loads of kids have tried over the years and every single one has failed for the weirdest reason. Even Tan had a go two years ago, before he was too old for the record.'

'He didn't make it?'

'Nope. He was caught in the net of a French fishing trawler near the south-west shipping lane. My dad was on the support boat and had practically followed them to Calais before they realized. He was found half-buried in a pile of mackerel. He's barely swum since.'

'That's unlucky,' said Casper. He couldn't decide whether Wynn was pulling his leg.

'Anyhow,' she continued. 'I'd better get a move on – my dad will be home by now and wanting to get to bingo. He's got his eye on a bathrobe set in tonight's prizes.'

'It was nice to meet you.' Casper smiled weakly, still unsure whether he should actually be worried by Wynn's warnings about swimming the Channel.

'I'll see you tomorrow!' she called, having hoisted her surfboard back under one arm. She jogged briskly over the dunes towards the heather and disappeared into the woodland.

Triton went back to tugging on his lead and pulled Casper down the sand. 'Where are you taking me?' he asked the little dog, who yipped in response – as if to say, *You'll see*.

After a few hundred metres, Triton came to an abrupt halt and Casper tripped awkwardly over his lead in surprise. They were standing in front of a short row of wooden beach huts, gnarly with age and nestled into the wild foliage behind where they were cradled like eggs in a nest of green and brown bracken. Dusting himself off, Casper looked up to see the number of a hut with scuffed pink doors.

702

He took the key he'd found in Ida's kitchen drawer from his pocket and read the writing on its keyring. '*Beach Hut 702* – Triton, you found it!' he cheered, rubbing the dog's head in delight. 'So, you have been down here before . . .'

Casper fussed over the dog with delight before Triton pulled towards the neighbouring hut with a low whimper. It was then that Casper noticed a woman sleeping on a stripy deck chair one cabin over, the green pastel doors of her hut pinned open. Her face was covered by a huge straw sun hat and her long dark limbs, splayed out to catch sunlight from every possible angle, glistened with layers of sun cream which smelt like coconut – even from a distance. A soft snore drifted from beneath the hat's wide brim.

'We'd better keep the noise down, Triton. We don't want to wake our neighbour.'

The dog answered with another sad whimper.

Casper lifted the door's huge padlock. It was caked in a thick layer of sharp, burgundy rust from countless years of rain and sea spray. Even so, the key slid inside and the mechanism ground open with a satisfying crunch. Casper pulled the double doors open with an exaggerated flourish and was immediately covered in a musty grey cloud of dust that sent him into a coughing fit.

'How long has this been locked?' he choked, batting away the dirt.

Triton leapt inside, and left a small trail of red pawprints wherever his feet picked up the grime. The rest of the carpet was black from years of dust having soaked into the fabric, and cobwebs covered every surface. Nevertheless, Casper yanked the stiff curtains closed and quickly changed into his swimming trunks.

The excitement of the sea filled him to bursting as he emerged back on to the seafront, a soft breeze warming his skin.

Casper tied Triton's lead to the door and the dog continued to clamber in the direction of their sleeping neighbour. 'Please be quiet,' he pleaded. 'I won't be long.'

The dog whimpered again, but Casper turned towards the beach and raced full pelt for the sea. The yellow sand slid smoothly across his webbed toes, which sank into the powder like enormous plastic spades. Without slowing for a second, he reached the water and splashed straight through the foamy surf unblinking. Heavy waves broke across his chest with a thrash. It was far colder than he would have ever anticipated, but Casper pushed on regardless – excitement overwhelming his senses. When the next wave approached, larger and taller than him even as he stood on his fleshy tiptoes, Casper dove into the water and disappeared.

Beneath the surface, he sailed through the misty blue like a rocket ship heading for the stars. The sea held him like an old friend, and for the briefest moment, every bit of frustration he'd ever felt on dry land washed away like a layer of sand.

It felt like home.

He turned towards the surface and kicked for the sunlight above, which suddenly seemed to be further away than his shallow depth should make possible. Before long he broke through the waves, gasping from effort and the shock of the cold sea on his body. Casper felt as though he couldn't find the air to fill his lungs quick enough. He gasped and gasped, searching for oxygen as frantically as his legs were now kicking to stay afloat. The cold water compressed his body.

Another wave crashed over his head, splashing his eyes which burned from the salt. In the distance he could hear Triton barking furiously. The sound came in and out of Casper's hearing – his face continuing to drop beneath the surface, the air no longer finding its way into his lungs. Elation turned to terror, and his parents' voices resounded in his head. Shouldn't he have listened to their warnings of the water? He'd been so foolish.

His weakened body failed to inhale, and struggled to keep him afloat. He dipped beneath the waves once again, and Casper watched as the sun flickered on the shimmering water above, which drifted only higher and further from his sinking, outstretched arms.

CHAPTER SIX

Beryl the Bazooka

The light continued to float further from Casper's fading view. He held his breath, refusing the persuasive urge to inhale a mouthful of the water now clouding his vision while the cold prickled his skin. Then, a tightness closed around his wrist. A sharp pull dragged him upwards. He was soaring away from the darkness, lifted towards the surface which broke in two as he burst through the water with a painful gasp.

The taste of salt burned in his throat, and he found that he was moving backwards through the sea, draped across the shoulder of someone who radiated strength. The dark water of the Channel sped past his vision in a blur and before he knew it, the dry sand was warming his skin as a familiar face looked down at him.

'Well, that weren't so smart now, was it?'

Beryl the Bazooka's pink mohawk was slick with water, which dribbled gently down her neck. She loomed over Casper, her long limbs lean and wrinkled but pulsating with the energy of someone half her age. She wore a white swimming costume which gleamed glossy with seawater, mirroring the brightness of her shiny false teeth. Her straw sun hat lay abandoned by the beach huts where it blew delicately down the sand. Triton, his lead taut, tried desperately to catch it in his jaws.

'What were you thinking, charging into the sea on your own like that? You would've drowned if it weren't for Triton waking me with his yapping.'

'You're— You're Beryl the Bazooka!' gasped Casper, his laboured breaths battling exhaustion and excitement. 'You're my hero!'

Beryl batted away his admiration with a wave of her skeletal fingers. 'Think nothing of it, kid. I would do the same for anyone.'

'No,' rasped Casper. 'You're literally my hero. I have all your newspaper clippings taped inside my wardrobe.'

Beryl raised an eyebrow.

'I mean, I've followed your whole career! I've read so much about you; every article since you broke the record for being the oldest person to swim the Channel at seventy-five. I've watched that news report a million times too. It's amazing! Swimming is my favourite thing in the world.'

'So you're a swimmer, eh?' she smiled, surveying the pale boy with scepticism. 'If you ask me, almost drowning seems to be a pretty funny technique.'

'Well,' Casper blushed again, the oxygen returning to the desperate corners of his body, 'I was taken by surprise. I've never actually been in the sea before, and—'

'You've never even been in the sea an' you go racing into the depths of the Channel on your first go?' laughed Beryl, exasperated. She held out a hand for Casper and pulled him to his feet, which were caked in sand – the webbings hidden from view. 'Let's get you into a deck chair and I'll pop the kettle on.'

Beryl helped Casper hobble back across the sand dunes, which seemed to roll along the seafront like lumpy, golden hills. The beach huts were now sinking low in the shade of the pine trees that rose behind, and Casper looked down the short line to see one other hut still occupied. Beside the pale blue doors of the furthest cabin there sat an ancient woman, who had to be close to a hundred years old. She was perched so impossibly still on the seat of an electric scooter, that Casper would have sworn it was driven by a stuffed vulture if the woman hadn't fixed him with such a steely gaze. Her skin rippled in the breeze like the surface of the sea, and her fine hair, thinner than a spider's silk, blew gently like the ghost of a girlish head of curls.

Casper felt a chill run down his spine as he returned her stare.

Bork!

He looked down to find Triton, who had bounded over the moment he could reach – his lead still stretched taut and his tail wagging furiously. The dog pawed gently at Casper's wet shins.

'I'm all right,' he beamed, forgetting the strange woman as he scratched Triton behind the ear. The dog licked his wrist with a rough tongue. 'Thank you for waking Beryl up, boy. You probably saved my life!'

'*Definitely* saved your life!' barked Beryl from inside her beach hut.

Casper untied Triton's lead in gratitude, and the wiry canine bounced across the yellow mounds towards the water.

'There,' exclaimed Beryl, propping up a second wooden deck chair. Casper sank into the stripy canvas with a sigh. The shock of his near-drowning was finally replaced by a dull ache which rippled through his muscles.

Inside, Beryl placed an old-fashioned kettle on a tiny stovetop, and pulled back the gingham curtains below to reveal a bulbous, orange bottle of gas. She fussed over the nozzle and after lighting a match, which she held to the hob, a dazzling blue flame burst into life and moisture crept up the sides of the steel kettle.

Casper peered around the pastel green doors and at the cosy room inside, its bright pink cabinets absorbing Beryl's neon hair in a mess of rosy colour.

She continued to potter about making tea, while Casper looked up at the ceiling. It was lined by long wooden poles that stretched the width of the beach hut, supporting an enormous selection of swimming aids, the sight of which lifted his spirits. A colourful assortment of fins lay beside foam pull buoys, over-sized plastic hand paddles and body boards in all shapes and sizes. On the wall hung a pair of goggles beside several wetsuits that glimmered like whale flanks, dripping water down on to the lid of a clear plastic tub. Casper saw that it was labelled 'goose fat' in scratchy biro and was filled with a thick, gelatinous-looking paste.

Suddenly embarrassed by the dusty state of Ida's beach hut, Casper stretched his left leg out and kicked the closest pink door shut with his massive toes.

'No need to worry about that mess,' said Beryl, appearing with a wooden tray. She sank into her deck chair and Casper hastily pulled his webbed feet in to hide them from view. Beryl was his idol and he'd only just met her; he couldn't risk her thinking he was a freak.

'Your gran hasn't been down here in a long while, I bet it's filthier than a fishwife's apron in there.' She handed him a tea. Casper took a sip and looked down at the mug to see a picture of a handsome merman on the side. He wore a French beret and a glass English monocle – the logo of the Channel Swimming Syndicate.

'You know my granny?' he asked, distracted.

'Ida?' Beryl replied. 'Of course; we've been beach hut neighbours for twenty-odd years! We used to be pretty darn close too.'

'Used to?'

'You must be her grandson, Casper,' said Beryl, ignoring the question.

'She told you about me?' he spluttered in amazement. 'But she can't have spent much time down here; it sounds like she hates the beach.'

Beryl smiled ruefully. 'Odd thing to keep a beach hut if you hate the beach.'

'That's what I thought!' said Casper, chewing this over in his mind. Perhaps Ida *did* like the sea, really, but knew his parents would disapprove ...

'Anyway,' started Beryl, dunking a piece of shortbread in her tea. She offered the packet to Casper, and he took one with delight. 'What were you doing running into the sea without another soul in sight?'

'I swim all the time,' boasted Casper. 'In ponds, fountains, puddles . . . any patch of water I can find!'

'Ponds and puddles?' Beryl asked, aghast. 'That's hardly the same as diving head first into a river or lake, let alone the freezing cold sea! The water is a powerful thing. You've got to show it some respect.'

Casper hung his head and Beryl softened.

'I suppose I can't be too hard on you,' she said. 'You've just arrived and Corallium is a peculiar place . . . It winds its way inside your soul, wraps itself tight and then never lets go.'

'People keep saying stuff like that.'

'Well, maybe it's true,' smiled Beryl. 'There must be a reason that this town is filled with energetic old fogies. We resist the call of the ocean for much of our lives, but eventually it grabs us by the throat, and we can't think of anythin' except being by the sea.'

'It's not just old fogies – that's exactly how I feel too,' blustered Casper, spitting shortbread crumbs across his swimming trunks. 'I've always dreamt of being here and now that I am, I don't have a second spare. I'll be twelve soon. I've only got a few weeks left!'

'Left for what?' asked Beryl, entertained.

Casper swallowed a mouthful of tea with an overly eager gulp, sending a painful ripple down the walls of his throat. His stomach somersaulted with a sudden show of insecurity. The memory of burning salt water returned to his nostrils, along with Wynn's promise of a Channel-swimming curse.

'I . . . I want to become the youngest person to ever swim the Channel.'

'Do you now?' answered Beryl, with an air of respect. Her eyes wandered down to the last beach hut in the row, where the strange woman's electric scooter had disappeared behind the flapping curtain which muffled the hushed voices mumbling inside. 'Quite the task you've set yourself there.'

'Well, it's all down to you. Like I said, you're my hero!'

Beryl perused her young new friend in a moment of thought. 'Some people place a lot of weight behind records and trophies . . . They don't think somethin's worth doing unless they're the best at doing it. Or the fastest. Or the *oldest*. Lots of kids your age have dreamt of besting Bernie's Channel record . . .'

'You know Baby Face Bernie?' cried Casper. He

remembered a black-and-white photo he'd found in the library's dusty book of world records. A chubby, cherub-like boy wearing an old-fashioned stripy one-piece swimming costume had smiled proudly, standing on the rocks on the coast of France.

'Aye, I know Bernie,' said Beryl. 'No one's broken that record for sixty years, and maybe they never will.'

Can that really be down to a curse? wondered Casper. He pushed the thought from his mind and dug his webbed feet into the sand, further sheltering them from view. 'I know that I can do it,' he said. 'I have a ... gift!'

'Is that so?' smiled Beryl, scratching her bright fuchsia scalp.

'Yes. I'm going to become the youngest person to *ever* swim the Channel!'

'Absolutely *out* of the question!' cried Granny Ida, appearing on the sand dunes behind them. She marched towards her long-abandoned beach hut and Triton bounced over, shaking his fur as sploshes of seawater showered her trench-coated shins.

'Granny!' yelped Casper in alarm. He had totally forgotten the time. It must've been ages since he'd sneaked from the house. 'I'm sorry, I was just taking Triton for a walk and—'

'You're coming home *now*,' she barked, her sternness at odds with her warm face and delicate curls.

Casper placed his mug on the table and shuffled towards his grandmother, taking care to keep his webbed toes covered by the sand with every step. 'It was brilliant to meet you, Beryl.'

'You too, kid,' she replied with a wink.

'We'll talk once you are home,' whispered Ida grimly. Casper gave her the beach hut key and collected his clothes and shoes. He smiled at Beryl in gratitude, before starting the walk back across the dunes and up through the woodland – Triton at his heels.

'You look well,' started Beryl, once Casper rounded the corner. Ida fumbled with the rusty padlock, finally sealing the beach hut from the waterfront and spinning around to face Beryl. The shadow of the words that she wanted to say were edging their way around her lips, and the women held each other's silent gaze. After the shortest of moments, Ida thought better of it and turned away. She began to trace her grandson's footsteps back along the beach, all the while hiding her face so that it would not betray the feelings of loss that were silently swelling inside her.

CHAPTER SEVEN

The Silhouette at Sunrise

Casper and his grandmother walked back through the woodland, their silence punctuated only by Triton's barks which echoed as he chased squirrels up and down the trail. Once the front door of Ida's draughty home had closed behind them a short while later, Casper finally found his courage. 'I'm really sorry for sneaking out, but I couldn't wait another second longer. I *had* to see the sea –

I couldn't stop myself!'

Ida untied the belt of her trench coat and hung it on the wooden stand, before assessing Casper with a sceptical squint.

'I've wanted to see it my whole life,' he continued. 'Being this close to the water, it's like a knot in my stomach has finally unravelled – one I didn't even know was pulled so tight. My parents have kept me away from here, and from the sea, for so long. They don't understand how swimming makes me feel...'

Ida gave a long, deep sigh – her face hidden for a second while she placed the beach hut key back inside the kitchen drawer. 'You'd be surprised,' she said curiously. 'I know how keen you are, but you can't sneak off without a soul knowing where you've gone. The sea is a dangerous thing. There are rip currents, and it's *cold* – even in the summer. I dread to think what could've happened if you'd rushed into the water and found yourself in trouble.'

Casper looked sheepishly at the floor, avoiding her eyes and failing to mention that this was exactly what had happened. 'I'm a great swimmer,' he said finally. 'And Beryl the Bazooka was there. That's even better than having an actual lifeguard on duty!'

Ida frowned, an involuntary tut leaving her tongue. 'Just promise me that you won't go near the water unsupervised again.'

'I prom— Wait a second,' beamed Casper. 'You mean I'm allowed to go back?' He saw his grandmother hesitate, her bottom lip quivering as her face flickered through a whole range of emotions.

'It would be cruel to stop you from going to the beach,' she said at last, her eyes glossy. 'It's so close after all. But I want you to promise me you'll stay out of the water. OK?'

The bubble of hope in Casper's chest burst with a belch. He'd finally made it to the sea, and was still banned. It was worse than he could have imagined.

'Casper, I know you think your parents are a bit extreme, but I'm sure there's a very good reason for their rules. All they want is for you to be safe.'

He looked up to his grandmother, silently crossing a pair of fingers behind his back as he wondered how much she really knew . . .

'I promise,' he lied.

That night, Casper lay wide-eyed in bed. Even after his near-drowning, the dreamlike hum of the waves drifting through his open window was so inviting. It called out, begging him to run back and dip his webbed toes in the foam.

When he finally managed to steal some sleep a few hours before sunrise, his thoughts were trained on the water. He dreamt he was in the open ocean, rolling across the buoyant waves like a bodyboard as his bright pink hair shone as brightly as a beacon on the surface. Beryl cheered from the deck of the RMS *Titanic*, which hovered beside him and pulled an inflatable banana boat – carrying both of his parents through the water. They were still fully bandaged and clung to the yellow rubber for dear life. Suddenly, the dream scene changed and his luminous barnet melted into a flashing dot on the screen of a GPS tracker. The pink dot moved closer and closer to the outline of France on the console's digital map of the English Channel . . .

Casper woke with a start, feeling a lacy imprint from his pillow etched in his cheek.

The dream played over in his mind.

How was he going to swim the Channel in just a few weeks' time? He'd been working towards this goal for so long, swimming lengths of every pond and fountain he'd ever found, even before he'd heard of Beryl and her record.

But Ida was right about one thing, at least. He would've been in real trouble if Beryl hadn't been there to drag him, and his webbed feet, from the freezing water. Casper hated having to lie, because even though his granny appeared to agree with his parents on the thing that mattered most to him . . . he really liked her.

A scratching noise drew Casper's attention to the hallway. A black nose appeared in the gap of the door, and before long Triton had squeezed his way through and bounded over.

'Hello, boy, what are you doing up here?' whispered Casper. The dog licked his hand affectionately and rolled on to his back, expecting attention – which Casper happily delivered with a scratch to the dog's belly. 'Couldn't you sleep either?'

Casper looked to the window and wondered how long it was until morning. He walked to the curtains, Triton at his heels, and after pulling them open he sighed in awe at the blackness of the sea. Even in the near-dark the water was somehow alluring. The sky was a purple bruise of colour, the earliest flecks of orange light now rising on the horizon like two wings of fire stretched wide. Casper's eyes followed the new colour as it sailed across the sea towards the empty shore, and then he realized . . .

The shore wasn't empty at all.

A dark figure stood in the shallows, where the water lapped quietly at their legs like the gentle paws of a friendly feline. The person's face, hidden in the half-light, was turned towards the sky in silent thought.

'Who is *that*?' Casper wondered aloud. The figure was unmoving, their silhouette an outline of tranquillity amid the toing and froing of the waves. Casper turned to Triton, who had hopped up on to the bed and curled himself into a sleepy pretzel. 'Who would be out there so early, Triton? They aren't even swimming, they're just . . . *standing* there.'

He turned back to the window, the orange glow intensifying.

'They've disappeared!' he cried out, covering his mouth in surprise at the volume. His eyes scanned the seafront back and forth, searching for the silhouette of a person, but found nothing. Triton yawned loudly and lay his head on a paw.

'I guess you're right,' continued Casper, allowing the curtains to fall shut. 'I'm probably just tired.'

He sloped back towards the bed, not really believing the comment but also not feeling as if he could trust his eyes. He crawled beneath the lacy sheets while Triton trotted up the mattress to collapse beside his head.

Moments later, they were both fast asleep.

Another hour passed before the summer sun had fully risen to stream through the curtains with a teasing promise of day. Overly warm, Casper woke again with a light sheen of sweat stuck to his forehead. Triton was gone.

Casper clambered from the bed as the sound of clattering plates and the smell of hot pastry and melted butter drew his attention to the open doorway.

He peered over the banister to the entrance hall below.

What the—

The ground floor was flooded. The polished tiles were hidden by a swirling pool of crystal water. Two large spirals churned in a clockwise direction like a sinking vortex, leading down into unknowable depths.

Casper stepped backwards, suddenly dizzy, but a strange feeling seemed to draw him down the stairs to the water. Slowly, he wobbled his way past the endless stream of blackened picture marks that lined the walls like ghosts from another person's life. His bare webbed feet slid smoothly along the corridor and once he reached the first-floor landing, he paused beside the hallway cupboard and leant across the banister.

The water was gone!

Casper ran down the final staircase in a frenzy, lifting each of his feet as fast as he possibly could before missing a step when his heel slipped on the edge of the glossy wood. He felt his weight pull him backwards and his body hit the ground, forcing him to skid to the bottom of the steps and land in a painful pile.

A large pair of fluffy slippers appeared next to his face.

'Casper! I didn't hear you get up,' said Ida, peering down at her grandson. She was holding a large pot of tea with a handle shaped like a mermaid's tail.

Triton bounced from the kitchen and over to Casper's feet which, he realized in horror, were bare.

He hurriedly pulled himself into a kneeling position, hiding his naked toes beneath his bottom.

'I've just woken up.' He faked a yawn. 'I'm still tired; I wasn't paying attention and tripped on the stairs.'

'Well, I've made some croissants if you'd like one.'

'I'm not sure I'm hungry yet,' said Casper, still feeling nauseous from his vision of the phantom whirlpool. Was it just another trick of the mind, like the large white sails he'd seen billowing from the windows?

'That's fine, we'll be going for lunch in a little while. Assuming you've not broken a bone, head back upstairs and wash. You probably still have sand in between your toes from yesterday.'

Knowing that the only thing in between his webbed toes was a thick band of flesh, Casper blushed as he looked towards the front door where the sun was streaming through the frosted glass.

'How do you expect me to wash?' he started, turning to Ida with a raised eyebrow. 'It's not even drizzling.'

Ida chuckled. 'I have the bath ready for you on the first floor. You'll find a warm towel in the airing cupboard opposite the bathroom, and I'll save a croissant for when you're done.'

'Bath?' Casper smiled.

'Yes, you silly thing. Now get upstairs!'

Casper bolted up the staircase and skidded to a halt outside the bathroom. He pulled back the shower curtain to find a free-standing porcelain bathtub, shimmering with water which gently steamed with an inviting mist. Grinning widely, he charged across the hallway to a cupboard and tugged on the handle.

Locked.

Why would Granny keep a secret cupboard inside her own home?

The question could wait – a bathtub was calling Casper's name. He found the airing cupboard one door over and pulled a fluffy towel from the bouncing pile, which cascaded to the floor behind him in a tidal wave of white cotton.

Without undoing so much as a single pyjama button, Casper leapt across the bathroom tiles and flew into the tub like a fully clothed flounder – a torrent of foamy water flooding the room.

CHAPTER EIGHT

The Many Misfortunes of Channel-Swimming Children

Casper and Ida wound their way along a narrow path of worn earth which cut through the lush, green clifftop gardens. Behind them the midday sun hovered over the craggy spires of Corallium Castle, which rose above the town like the hand of a sleeping giant.

Casper could hear the sea far below them as it

bashed against the rocks with a fervour. He felt the familiar quickening of his heart, and his webbed toes wriggled knowingly.

The water was still calling.

It was all he could do not to leap from the cliff's edge and roll right into the sea.

But just then, a building appeared on the horizon among the jagged earth as though it were being pushed up through the ground itself. A hotel! A wind-battered white block of windows, covered in thirsty green vines and thick tree roots which rippled around its lower floors like searching fingers. Though it shone as brightly as a set of teeth, the building was half-swallowed by the landscape.

A long gravel driveway ran from the mouth of the building and around a large fountain beside the cliff face. There, Casper saw another small structure perched on the edge. It looked like a tiny train station, though strangely its track appeared to drop straight down the precipice to certain doom.

'Granny, what's a railway doing on the side of a cliff?' asked Casper.

'That's the funicular,' said Ida. 'There's no path to the seafront this far along, so it works like a very steep railway – only with small single carriages, rather than trains.'

Casper's eyes widened as one of these carriages rose into view. It crested the edge of the cliff face and came to a stop inside the tiny station. The funicular seemed to defy the rules of gravity.

'There are two cars,' continued Ida. 'They're attached to opposite ends of one cable and as one comes up the track, the other goes down. Right now, the other car will be reaching the seafront.'

That was all that Casper needed to hear for him to sprint directly to the station. A handful of women were waiting to board, each one clutching a sun hat tightly to their head for fear of the breeze. Several held collapsed deck chairs and towels beneath their arms.

'Excuse me,' panted Casper. He squeezed his way through the queue to get as close to the emptying car as possible, hoping that he might be able to look directly down the track. The funicular rails ran straight down the cliff, cutting a clear path through the woodland. At the very bottom, the crystal blue waters of the Channel shimmered invitingly.

'Casper, this way!'

He turned to see Ida standing beneath the glass canopy at the hotel entrance. Reluctantly, Casper pulled himself away from the sea and trundled over to the hotel. Its name was emblazoned above the revolving doorway in chipped emerald lettering:

L'HÔTEL PERLE

The enormous sign had a large white orb set in the centre of the 'Ô' which shimmered with an oily sheen. The entire building looked as if it might've washed up on the coast after a devastating storm.

'I love this town,' said Casper, staring at the building in awe.

'I'm so pleased to hear that,' Ida replied with a genuine smile.

'I could just about believe that it really was all once on the bottom of the sea – though I know it sounds stupid,' he added quickly, seeing Ida's frown.

'You've heard about that?' she asked.

'Just in passing. Can you tell me some of the stories?'

'It's just a silly made-up thing for the tourists,' she said, clearing her throat and batting the subject away.

Casper squinted.

If they're just silly stories, why do they seem to bother

Granny so much?

'Let's get inside,' she said. 'I'm starving.'

The entrance of the hotel was a dimly lit corridor lined with glass cases, each one filled with peculiar trinkets. As they walked through, Casper noticed a row of razor-sharp shark teeth, a selection of ancient coins and cutlery, and an enormous brass trident that took up the entire length of one cabinet. Beyond was a bustling dining room, from which the chink of glasses and the scratching of silverware on china plates echoed down the hallway. The tables inside were shaped like emerald oyster shells, each one surrounded by elderly diners who were slowly eating Sunday lunch.

'Casper!'

His eyes scanned the sea of blue hair and silk scarves. Finally, he spotted a long dark plait attached to a familiar face. Wynn rushed over.

'I'm so glad you're here! Please save me and Tan from our dad. He won the bingo last night and made some enemies in the process.' She motioned to a table in the centre of the room. A middle-aged man with brown skin and wavy black hair sat next to a boy who was his younger double. Despite their age gap, the biggest difference between Wynn's brother and father was that her dad was wearing a bright pink bathrobe.

'He's a really bad winner,' Wynn continued, as if to explain the strange outfit.

'And who's this?' said Ida, appearing beside them and surprising Casper with the reminder of her presence.

'Oh, sorry. Wynn, this is my granny, Ida. Ida, this is my new friend, Wynn.'

'A new friend already? We've only been here two minutes.'

'We met at the beach,' said Wynn. 'Casper said you have a hut down there, but I don't think I've ever seen you. Don't you use it?'

Casper felt his grandmother stiffen as the question hung in the air. Thankfully, at the same moment, Wynn's father grabbed the attention of the entire room with a bellow.

'Elsie, let *go*!'

The group turned to see him tussling with a short, squat woman. She sported a head of tight white curls and wore a huge pair of glasses attached to a chain around her neck.

'Elsie, I've told you,' said Wynn's dad, exasperated. 'I won this bathrobe fair and square. It's mine and that's the end of it.'

'I had bingo too, Dev,' shrieked Elsie, hitting the man on the head with a walking stick. 'I was about to call it when you swooped in and beat me to it.'

'Beat you to it, precisely!' howled Wynn's father, tearing the corner of his bathrobe from the woman's grip. Tan slid down his seat, mortified, while Elsie looked aghast. She spotted the pink cotton belt around Dev's waist and tore it from the loopholes, snatching it up into a ball in her fist before she could be stopped.

'Consider this *my* share!' she shrieked. Elsie spun on her heel and stomped back across the dining hall, draping the belt around her neck as she went and flicking it across one shoulder like a thin fluffy scarf.

Wynn turned to Casper and Ida with desperate eyes. 'Please sit with us,' she pleaded. 'That was just the tip of the iceberg. Before you arrived he was parading around the room like a king, inviting people to stroke his fuzzy arm.'

'I imagine your father would like a quiet lunch with his children—' started Ida, just as Wynn's dad once again leapt up from his seat.

'Let that be a lesson to you all!' he cried, folding the bathrobe tightly at his waist with a curt nod.

'Please?' begged Wynn.

'We'd love to!' Casper grinned, before his granny could say another word.

Wynn's father, Dev Basu, was an enthusiastic man. His wavy black hair framed a kind face with deep-brown eyes, which were only brightened by the fluorescent pink bathrobe.

'What a treat to have you join us for lunch,' he said, after Casper and Ida had each been served a plate of questionable food. 'I'm so happy Wynn has made a young friend down here. I was getting worried!'

'That's hardly my fault. Even you two are young for Corallium,' she said with a huff, motioning to her dad and Ida. 'No offence,' she added with a guilty frown.

'None taken,' Ida laughed. 'Though Casper is only here for the summer, sadly. Once his parents are out of the hospital he'll be back to Bramble-in-the-Oaks.'

'Hospital?' asked Dev. 'I hope it's nothing serious.'

As Granny explained, Casper felt a stab of guilt at the thought of his mum and dad laid up in their beds.

They'd always said that keeping him from the water was for his safety. He'd thought they were overreacting, but what if they'd been right? He'd spent one day in Corallium and had already almost died!

'The doctors say they'll be up and about in a few weeks,' Ida was saying. 'But it was a surprise to learn how much damage a cheese can do ...'

Casper prodded a brown, gelatinous piece of meat that wobbled on his plate. 'What's with this meal?' he whispered to Wynn.

'Kidneys and boiled potatoes,' she replied. 'What were you expecting in a town with an average age of eighty-one?'

Wynn plugged her nose with a pinch and swallowed a mouthful. Casper's eyes skimmed the room and spotted a table of diners, who each removed a set of false teeth before tucking into their meals. He shuddered, licking his own teeth to make sure they were still fixed in place.

'Smoked mackerel was the other option,' said Wynn, spotting his displeasure. 'I'd have probably ordered that, but my brother still can't stand the smell after ...'

Casper looked across the table at Tan. His loose

black waves gave a breezy, beachy vibe which was a stark contrast to his expression – a picture of grumpy irritation. He stabbed his food with a fork in between frowns.

'You mean that story about the mackerel boat was true?' asked Casper, under his breath. 'I thought you were making fun of me with that stuff about a curse.'

'Of course not,' Wynn replied. 'I would never lie about that, it was awful. Tan was desperate to swim the Channel. He trained for ages and would've made it, if not for that net plucking him from the sea like an arcade crane machine.'

'But it was an accident, right?' said Casper.

'Are you talking about me?'

Casper and Wynn looked up to find Tan glaring at them.

'Um—'

'Wynn was just saying you're a brilliant swimmer,' said Casper quickly, saving his friend from her brother's ire. 'I'm a swimmer too.'

'Casper is going to swim the Channel this summer,' Wynn added bluntly.

Tan's face turned to stone.

'Swimming the Channel? Now that's a goal and a

half, good for you!' said Dev cheerfully, joining their conversation. 'You must have had that slot booked for years? Lots of people come to Corallium and make that crossing. The swell is good here and helps wash you right across the separation zone. I bet you'll be eating a croissant by sunrise!'

'Er,' stuttered Casper. *Slot booked?* What did he mean?

'You're a little lean for a long-distance swimmer,' continued Dev. A waiter appeared to collect several empty serving dishes which had been piled high with soggy cabbage. 'Tan here is the perfect build, and would've broken Bernie's record if it weren't for that ridiculous thing with the mackerel boat.'

'Dad,' started Tan, his face a deep crimson. Casper's heart ached for him.

'What sort of times are you clocking?' continued Dev, ignoring his son's embarrassment. 'I'll bet you've got your six-hour sea swim in the can . . . Is that the longest you've swum so far?'

Casper slipped down his seat until his chin was almost on the table. This was overwhelming. No one had ever shown the slightest bit of interest in his swimming, and now he realized just how unprepared and amateur he'd seem to anyone with knowledge of the task ahead. He couldn't exactly tell them about his secret weapon . . .

His webbed feet.

'I think Casper was teasing you, Wynn,' said Ida. She swallowed a mouthful of potato which she'd mashed with the back of her fork. 'This is the first time he's visited the seaside, so he'd need quite a bit more practice if he wanted to swim the Channel.'

She smiled warmly, ending the conversation with a full stop.

Casper noticed that Tan's stony expression had fractured into the fine lines of a handsome smirk, aimed squarely at him.

'Dev, tell us more about your bingo victory,' Ida said, changing the subject. 'I haven't seen Elsie that angry since she lost a set of steel cookware to Judith Chambers at bowls.'

As Dev launched into his story, Casper pushed an unappealing piece of meat around his plate. Before long it was soggy with sauce and glistening like a squashed slug.

'What does she mean?' whispered Wynn, ignoring the adults. 'Are you not really swimming the Channel?'

'I am,' he blushed. 'I just don't have much time, and I've no idea where to start. Especially with my granny so against the idea.'

Wynn smiled, understanding. She turned to her father and Ida. 'We're going to look at the desserts,' she said. 'We'll be back in a minute.'

They crossed the dining room towards a silver trolley loaded with large bowls. Casper eyed the selection of sloppy, soft desserts and his stomach groaned sadly.

'Sorry about your gran,' Wynn started. 'Sometimes grown-ups just don't get it. We're capable of so much more than they know, if only they'd give us the chance to show them.'

'Exactly!' cheered Casper, buoyed by the unfamiliar show of support.

'It's probably best to save the swim until you're older anyway,' continued Wynn. She picked up a wibbly blancmange and jiggled the plate. 'You could start planning now for next year. That way you'll have plenty of time.'

'But I'll be twelve soon,' insisted Casper. 'To break the record I need to swim this summer!'

'I told you, that record is *cursed*.' Wynn waved her

fingers dreamily in front of Casper's face. 'You don't want to risk it. There's no telling what might happen to you . . . Look at my brother! He's traumatized by an oily fish.'

'But *how* can a record be cursed?'

'I don't know, but every kid that's tried to break it has failed miserably. My brother got off lightly, if you ask me – some others have had horrible accidents.'

'Like who?'

'Samuel Seabury. He lathered himself in goose fat and stepped into the sea before the sun had even risen. Forty-five minutes later, he was flat on his back on board the pilot boat with suspected hypothermia! Someone had replaced his tub of goose fat with thick Vaseline – great for dry skin, but completely useless in staving off the cold. He fully recovered, but now can't stand to feel anything less than room temperature. He never had another spot again, though, and moved to Milan. He's a world-famous skincare model now—'

'That's ridiculous,' said Casper, though he felt the hairs on his arm stand on end.

'What about Julia Bellwether?' continued Wynn as she fumbled with a small bowl of tapioca pudding. 'She made good progress on her swim, but after she entered the north-east shipping lane a woman tumbled from the top deck of a cruise liner. She was a socialite, with a first-class ticket to Madagascar! Her heavy jewellery sent her sinking to the bottom of the sea like a lead anchor in platinum earrings. Julia abandoned her swim to rescue her . . . The very moment she'd touched another person, she was disqualified. That was two days before her twelfth birthday.'

Casper exhaled deeply. He looked across the room to his granny and Dev, who was waving a pair of pink slippers in the air. Wynn's stories had done nothing to deter Casper from his goal, but they *had* made it clear just how urgent the task was.

And how little time was left.

'Beryl will help me,' he said with confidence.

'Beryl the Bazooka?' asked Wynn.

'She's my hero. I met her yesterday, when she saved me from—' Casper stopped short, embarrassed to admit that he had almost drowned in the middle of a conversation about how he planned to swim the Channel.

'Saved you from what?'

'It doesn't matter, but I know she'll help me prepare. The sea is in my blood. I can't explain how I know it, or why I feel this way, but this is something that I'm *meant* to be doing.'

'All right, Ariel. If it's what you want, then who am I to stop you? But when you're shooting your first campaign for Vaseline, remember me, won't you?' She smiled playfully, handing him a bowl of blancmange.

'Deal,' he laughed.

CHAPTER NINE

An Encounter with the Crone

Once the group had polished off dessert, Ida and Dev were served coffee dark as treacle. Casper and Wynn were happy to seize their wafer-thin chocolate mints, which came in individual paper sleeves like tiny, crinkled blankets.

'I imagine you two will want to get down to the beach?' asked Dev, causing Casper's webbed feet to silently fizz with excitement.

'I-I don't know about that,' stuttered Ida. 'Casper only got here yesterday. I think he should rest this afternoon and save some energy.' Despite it being well established that Ida didn't hold much love for the seafront, Casper was disappointed.

'Nonsense,' said Dev with a smile. 'There's not much else to do in Corallium. Everybody comes for the water, because they know that it's special here.'

'Is it true that you're researching Corallium's ancient origin?' Casper asked.

'I told you, that's just a story,' said Ida, fidgeting awkwardly with a strand of hair which had fallen from behind her ear.

'Oh, it's not,' countered Dev, his face alight with enthusiasm. 'Just look around you – this town is soaked in history. The streets are lined with the ghosts of shellfish who would once have called the ground beneath our feet the ocean floor . . . Look at Corallium Castle! You can't tell me you think it was built from stone and rock by human hands?'

Ida shifted uncomfortably while Casper leant forward, hooked on every word. Wynn pretended to fall asleep, having heard it all a million times before, and Tan continued to scowl.

'I'm currently excavating a small section of land beneath the castle,' Dev continued. 'The rock is incredible – gabbro and basalt, in formations that you'd expect to find in the ocean crust! You must get Wynn to bring you down for a visit, Casper, there is just so much to see.'

'I'd love that!' Casper cheered.

'I feel like I'm on the brink of an enormous discovery. Something that will help me prove that Corallium was once an underwater city, home to an ancient race of sea folk!'

Ida choked on a mouthful of coffee, spluttering brown liquid into her napkin while Casper slapped her gently on the back.

'Thank you,' she said, once she'd recovered. 'You know what, perhaps you two should head to the beach after all.'

Casper felt lighter than ever as he walked through the hotel with Wynn, even if it did seem like Granny had only let him go to shut down the conversation *again*.

'I don't think your brother likes me much,' he said to Wynn, seeing Tan's surly face glaring from the table.

'I wouldn't take it personally,' she smiled. 'All that talk about swimming the Channel probably brought back memories of when he couldn't – or didn't, I should say. He definitely *would've* if it weren't for the curse.'

Casper shook his head. The curse, again. How could he take Wynn's tales of Vaseline and platinum earrings seriously? Surely Tan and the mackerel boat was just a freak accident.

It had nothing to do with Casper.

Arriving outside, the pair were greeted by a wall of heat which was amplified by the glass canopy like a magnifying lens. Casper's chubby toes swelled with longing at the sound of the splashing water as it gushed from the fountain in front of the building.

'Can we take the funicular?' he asked, desperate to reach the shore as quickly as possible.

'OK,' said Wynn. 'I'll show you the heather walk. Ooh, and there's a spooky cave that my dad says might've been where sirens once called sailors to their grisly deaths.' Casper gulped, and Wynn smiled with devilish excitement. 'Let's go!'

They bounded over to the boxy station which jutted from the greenery like a birder's hideaway, nestled among the long grass and vegetation of the sheer woodland slope. At the entrance, a small metal turnstile led the pair to the top of the track which seemed to slide away into nothingness. The sea crashed loudly against the sand below.

'Two, is it?' asked a man inside the ticket office. He wore glasses thicker than the cold blancmange that Casper had forced down after lunch, and the hair sprouting from his ears was as white as sea foam. The man sat stiffly inside the small kiosk and held a rusty ticket machine which he wound like an accordion to produce two small paper tickets. Casper saw that his name tag read: *Wilbur*.

'That'll be three shillings.'

'Shillings?' asked Casper, mystified. He'd heard of a shilling, but thought it was a very old type of money that hadn't been used in decades.

'Thank you,' interrupted Wynn. She passed Wilbur three dull silver coins and took the stubby tickets, handing one to Casper.

'Thanks,' he said.

'You'll need to visit the money exchange,' Wynn instructed. 'The only currency they take around here is shillings, farthings, and sometimes even old stamps.'

'Where's the money exchange?' asked Casper, more baffled by this town than ever.

'He's a guy called Chester. You'll find him sitting on a bench by the castle every first and third Thursday of the month.'

Casper wasn't sure if Wynn was joking, but his next question was swallowed by distraction when he caught a glimpse of blue in the corner of one eye. He craned his neck around the kiosk and stared straight down the funicular tracks towards the water, which was tantalizingly close.

'Step back,' cried Wilbur with a craggy squeal. 'Watch yerselves now.'

Wynn pulled Casper back behind the barrier as one of the cars slowly juddered up the slope on its way into the station. With its rusty roof of chipped blue paint, Casper could have believed that someone had stuck wheels on a garden shed before attaching it to the side of the cliff. The car stuttered to a halt and the ticket attendant hobbled across to the chain metal door which slid open stiffly like an elevator cage. A dozen women, all in their seventies, hopped quickly from the cabin. They each wore flowery swimsuits which covered from wrist to ankle, sporty white running trainers and large swimming goggles which magnified their eyes to the size of china saucers.

'OK, ladies,' a plump woman called from the front while jogging neatly on the spot. 'Are we all ready?'

'Mabel, have we time for a quick group photo on the cliff?' asked a lady near the back.

'Don't be silly; we're on course for a personal best! Now, on your marks . . . Get set . . . GO!'

Suddenly the whole group were sprinting through the tall grass on their way towards the castle. Casper stared, open-mouthed.

'There's definitely something in the water here,' said Wynn.

'In yer get, then,' croaked Wilbur.

Casper and Wynn crouched under his arm and hopped on board the funicular. Inside it was even warmer, so they quickly set about opening the slatted windows to let in as much air as possible. After they'd perched on a bench in the middle of the car, the shed on wheels began to slowly roll towards the cliff's edge as a large wheel attached to the side of the station spun them forward.

'I've not been on this for ages,' said Wynn. 'My dad

has refused to ride it ever since it malfunctioned once when we were halfway up. The car was stuck for an hour, and we missed the hotel's early bird special by two minutes. It was Spam day – he was fuming!'

Despite its age, the funicular rolled smoothly down the cliff face like a water slide in slow motion. The cab sank low into the trees of the woodland, where knobbly brown branches and glossy green stalks gently stroked the nearside window like a warm hello. Looking forward, Casper could see the blue water teasing through their tunnel-like view, as well as the second car which was rising from the seafront in tandem with their movement like the other side of a see-saw.

'There're probably people in that one too,' said Wynn, following Casper's line of vision. 'Let's wave when we pass!'

Casper joined her at the left-hand window, which faced the funicular's sister rail and another wall of trees behind. Suddenly, daylight was snuffed from the cabin as the thick woodland overtook them on all sides, and once the twin carriage was about to pass by the two friends began to wave excitedly.

'Oh, no,' cried Wynn, grabbing Casper's hand from

the air and pulling it down. She backed away from the window and crouched on the floor.

'What?' asked Casper, quickly realizing that he wouldn't need an answer.

The funicular car on its way up towards L'Hôtel Perle had just one passenger inside. Casper felt a shiver run down his spine when he saw the ancient woman sitting on her chunky motorized scooter. Her shadowy eyes were firmly closed. Her skin was wrinkled like a piece of screwed-up paper. She sat so still that even her threadlike curls were disturbingly static as the cab rolled by with every window shut tightly to the breeze.

'I know that woman,' whispered Casper.

In the very same moment, the crone's eyes snapped open and found his face from across the divide. A muffled scream escaped Casper's lips and Wynn pulled him down to the floor with a thump.

'That's Baby Face Bernie's mum,' Wynn said in a hushed voice. 'Agatha.'

'Bernie's *mum*?' Casper gasped, understanding that the woman must be even older than he'd thought. 'I saw her at the beach yesterday. She was staring at me when I left the sea with Beryl, then she just . . . disappeared.'

'Probably inside a beach hut. Bernie has one.'

Despite the wall of steel between them, Casper couldn't help feeling as though Agatha's eyes were burning right through the metal into his back. He risked lifting his head above the window for a look and found that the two cabs had already passed each other – Agatha's now rising slowly up to the clifftop station. Casper found her shape in the window and was horrified to see her ashen eyes still pointing directly towards him.

'Why is she always staring at me?' he wondered aloud with a large gulp.

'No idea, but she gives me the creeps. I don't envy Bernie, still putting up with her at his age. I wouldn't be surprised to learn that she hangs from the living room ceiling while she sleeps.'

'You know Bernie too?' asked Casper. He tore his eyes from Agatha's car, which had almost reached the station.

'Not personally, but he's pretty hard to avoid.'

'What do you mean?'

'You'll find out,' she said with a smirk.

Casper was about to push the question, but the cabin was suddenly filled with bright and brilliant sunlight. The funicular had rolled from the cloak of the woodland and was passing through the purple fields of heather. The familiar golden sand dunes rose ahead, blocking the water Casper had seen from the cliffs, and the car finally came to a halt in another small station – a mirror image of the one in which they'd boarded.

Casper looked back up the track to see the other car arriving at the top of the cliffs. It was too high up to be sure, but he would have sworn that he could still feel the cold and hardened stare of Agatha's eyes boring into his skin.

CHAPTER TEN

Les Moules-Frites

Casper and Wynn made their way along the heather walk, kicking up sand while they followed the narrow trail weaving its way through the brush like a yellow brick road.

'This path will lead us around the woodland and over to the beach huts,' said Wynn.

'Have you ever seen an adder?' asked Casper, wary of what the purple flowers might conceal. On cue, a tall stalk rocked in the breeze as though a lengthy body might be snaking its way across the root.

'One or two. Most of the time they're only grass snakes, but either way they're more scared of us than we are of them. They'd much rather slither off in the heather and hide than confront you. Just be careful where you're walking.'

Casper began to scan the trail with every step, walking as if he feared a landmine might explode underfoot at any second.

Once the path opened out, he finally looked up and took in the scene. To his right, the thick woodland climbed up the sloping cliffs like fuzzy green hands clawing the earth, reaching for the small town above with brown fingers. To his left, the purple heather continued to roll along the beach before scattering into clusters of thirsty yellow grass that dotted the dunes like clumps of dry spaghetti. As his eyes followed their rolling shape of peaks and valleys, a very odd sight came into view on one of the taller mounds in the distance.

A tugboat!

But . . . how? The sea was thirty metres away, past the dunes and behind a long stretch of golden beach.

Even if the tide were in, the boat would be lucky to touch the water, let alone set sail on it, but here it was, cresting an enormous swell of speckled sand.

'Wynn,' he asked, scratching his head with a scrunched-up hand. 'Is there a boat stranded on that sand dune, or am I seeing things?'

His mind travelled back to the vision of a swirling pool flooding Ida's entrance hall, and the billowing white sails which he'd seen above her house the previous day.

'You've not gone doolally, don't worry. That's *Les Moules-Frites*!'

The boat's white hull was packed tightly in the grassy dunes like a heavy-bottomed plant pot, and sure enough, Casper could see curly letters which spelt out *LES MOULES-FRITES* in silver paint.

Hanging from the side of the boat like rubber fenders was a long line of colourful china plates, each one picturing a delicately painted mythical sea crea-ture. On deck was what looked to be a small country cottage, with pale pink walls and royal-blue shutters which were open on to shiny sash windows. The flat roof of the miniature home was overflowing with a medley of terracotta pots which held a variety of plants and flowers, creating a sumptuous garden that seemed to float above the beach like a jungle paradise. At the very centre, a crooked brown chimney coiled delicately from the vegetation like a curious worm searching for sunlight. It billowed a cheery white smoke which floated up to form the only cloud in the otherwise clear blue sky.

'Isn't she a beaut?' said Wynn.

'She's a she?' asked Casper, still eyeing the tugboat home with great wonder.

'All boats are female,' said Wynn. 'It's tradition! In the olden days sailors thought that if they gave their ships a feminine name, in honour of their mothers or the gods, then it might help protect their passage and guide them safely home.'

'But why is there a ship on the dunes in the first place?' Casper's eyes landed on a thin washing line which ran between the back of the cottage and a flag-pole at the stern of the boat. Three flowery swimming caps hung from the wire beside a pair of plastic flippers, and at the top of the pole a striped rainbow flag blew proudly in the breeze.

'Well, it doesn't sail any more. It's Beryl's house.'

'Beryl the Bazooka?!' Casper exclaimed.

'That's my name, don't wear it out!' came a sharp voice. Casper looked up to find the bubblegum head of Beryl poking through one of the tugboat's open windows. 'Are you two gonna stand there gawping, or are you coming inside for a cuppa?'

The friends scrambled up the dunes to the tugboat, where Casper followed Wynn across a wooden beam that led to the main deck. They tiptoed in single file with their arms stretched wide for balance, while the nearest china plates shook against the hull with every wobble of the plank. Once they made it aboard they ran down to the stern of the boat and the front door of the cottage, where they ducked below the line of wet swimming caps and went inside.

'Whoa,' Casper breathed.

They were standing in the centre of a tiny lounge, where squidgy green armchairs circled a small coffee table in the shape of a clamshell. Pasted across the walls were overlapping maps of the world in all different sizes. Casper could see that inky dotted lines had been marked across each one, spanning the stretches of water that Beryl must have swum. One side of the room housed a small kitchenette and at the other, the ship's helm, a wooden steering wheel was set in front of the large window looking on to the bow. At the centre of the wheel was a carving of a merman, who held a long trident which extended up to form the central handle – upon which hung a pair of Beryl's frilly knickers.

'You like my home, then?' she asked, turning off the kettle.

'It's the most amazing place I've ever seen,' gushed Casper, desperately searching the room for every last detail.

'Shucks,' laughed Beryl. 'It's just a place to rest my pink head after a long day's swimmin'. I used to spend some time on the cliffs, but . . . I prefer it down here. I like to be as close to the water as possible.'

She ushered the children towards the armchairs and sat down in front of them with a tray of mugs and a steaming pot of tea. While she poured the drinks, Casper gazed at the world maps which stretched across the walls like creeping ivy. Above a small spiral staircase, which he thought must lead down to Beryl's bedroom, Casper recognized the route across the English Channel – the very same map which was stuck in his wardrobe at home. A faint pen line marked the zigzag route, which started metres from where he now sat in Corallium and ran across the water to a small spot on the bumpy northern coast of France.

Wynn followed his gaze. 'When it's up on the wall like that it seems like a long way to swim,' she frowned.

'I can manage it,' huffed Casper, slightly bruised. 'I just need to get training if I'm going to make the crossing this summer.'

Maybe now was the time to ask for help from the Bazooka.

He watched as Beryl sat back and sipped her tea, which was held by another one of her many mugs bearing the Channel Swimming Syndicate logo. She frowned. 'Casper told you about his near-drowning last night, then?'

'You almost *drowned*?' screamed Wynn.

Casper turned a deep shade of magenta. 'It was an accident; I wasn't ready for the cold. Now I know what I'm getting into, I'll be way more prepared.' He felt his webbed toes twitch inside his thick shoes at the thought. 'I still can't explain it, to either of you *or* myself . . . but I was born to be in the sea. I just know it!'

'Your gran was the same,' sighed Beryl. 'She was always saying that the sea was in her soul, passed down through her family for generations.'

'That's exactly it!' cheered Casper. 'But . . . that makes no sense. Why is she against me swimming if she feels the same way? And my parents, they hate the water. I didn't inherit any love for the sea from them, either.'

'Some people feel the need to fight against what comes naturally,' said Beryl. 'They push the offending thoughts right down to the bottom of their legs an' attempt to forget . . . But those thoughts are always there, niggling at them while they walk around all day with an annoying stone stuck inside their shoe as a reminder.'

Casper thought hard, imagining what could have possibly caused his family to take the drastic action of barring the ocean from their lives. Did they really feel the same longing he did? The same obsession that found him spending much of the day dwelling on nothing but the thought of dipping his toes back in the water? Granny lived just a few hundred metres up the woodland path. How could she keep herself away if what Beryl said was true?

'Don't get me wrong, this is lovely,' said Wynn. 'But, Casper, you only have a few weeks to break the record and *you almost drowned!* Tan trained for months and months, and he still didn't make it. Even if there wasn't a curse, maybe it's not such a good idea after all.'

Beryl chuckled. 'You've told Casper about the curse of the Channel-swimmin' children, eh, Wynn?'

Casper rolled his eyes. 'Just a load of rubbish about a woman sinking to the bottom of the sea because of her platinum earrings. Oh, and some kid that grew up to be a famous skincare model.' He scoffed.

'Oh, yes, Sammy Seabury – what a sweetheart,' Beryl gushed. 'His mother an' I were good friends. She still sends me his magazine clippings.' She rummaged in the carpet bag at her feet and lifted out a thick catalogue, which she threw on the table with a thud.

Casper pulled it towards him and turned to a page which was marked with a crumpled yellow post-it note. There, he found a full-page advert for something called Trésor de la Mer moisturizer. There was a picture of a young man wearing designer swimming trunks and a fancy pair of goggles. His entire body was smothered in cream, and his luminous skin glowed softly like a set of freshly laundered pillows.

'Tre-sor-de-la-mare,' Casper muttered.

'Expensive stuff,' said Beryl, snatching back the catalogue and tossing it towards a pile of boxes in the corner. They overflowed with unopened tubes of moisturizer, each one plastered with a pouting Samuel Seabury on the side.

'OK, so there've been a few accidents,' said Casper. 'That doesn't mean it's down to some horrible curse.'

'Then explain what happened to Jeremy Jones,' Wynn insisted.

'Ah, yes,' said Beryl. 'He was a real golden boy back in the eighties. He won every swimmin' gala going. The trouble was, he had this long blonde mullet. It went right down to his backside! Far too fashionable for his own good, if you ask me.'

Wynn nodded. 'I heard that he'd almost reached France when his support boat swerved off course. Jeremy was busy swimming, face down in the water, so didn't notice when the boat came too close. His mullet was so long that it floated back into the boat's propellor blades and—'

'His hair was churned up like a tin of old corned

beef,' added Beryl. 'He was so distraught to lose those ratty locks that he couldn't carry on swimmin''

'His hair wouldn't fit inside a swimming cap,' Wynn explained.

'That's ridiculous,' sighed Casper.

'It's the truth!' she shouted, with her arms in the air. 'Tell him, Beryl.'

'Oh, it's the truth, all right. That boy was balder than my great-uncle Boney Bob once that propellor blade was through with him. He never swam again, bless him. Couldn't face it. Too many bad memories!'

'Just like my brother,' said Wynn.

Casper had heard enough. Every moment that he spent listening to idiotic stories was another one wasted. He should be in the sea, dedicating every spare second he had to training. He had wanted this for far too long to let it go to waste.

'Thank you for the tea, Beryl,' he said, standing up. 'But I really need to get swimming.'

'Come on, Casper,' Wynn smiled. 'Drink up and we can talk it all through.'

'I don't want to drink any more tea; I want to be out *there*, in the water.'

'But, Casper—'

'You don't understand!' he cried, heading for the front door of the tugboat cottage. 'You haven't been stuck in the middle of nowhere all your life, never even having glimpsed the sea before yesterday. I've only seen it in my dreams, which feel like they're pulled from someone else's memory. Swimming is all I've ever wanted to do, and I've been kept from doing it at every possible turn . . . My parents were hit by that wheel of cheese for a reason. I was sent *here* for a reason!'

Beryl and Wynn shared a look of bewilderment, and the pensioner mouthed 'Cheese?' with a frown.

Casper threw the cottage door open and made his way on to the deck of the boat. 'I need to do this. I *need* to satisfy this hunger that's inside me. I'm going to swim the English Channel and I'm going to become the youngest person to ever do it!'

'Is that right?' came a sneering voice.

Casper looked down over the tugboat's railing.

Standing at the top of the sand dunes, beside an ancient woman on a motorized scooter, was a figure Casper had seen countless times before in the black-and-white photo from inside the book of world records. The chubby child from the picture may have grown into a gangly old man, but he was still instantly recognizable.

It was Baby Face Bernie.

And he looked furious.

CHAPTER ELEVEN

Baby Face Bernie

Bernie's boyish hair was somehow still the same mop of blonde curls, which should have belonged to a child a fraction of his age. It bounced with each of his angry outward breaths like a bag of yellow candyfloss.

His scrawny limbs, a shadow of the stocky boy Casper had seen in pictures, were wrapped in a dusty-looking swimming costume several sizes too small –

an all-in-one stripy number, with a fussy collar that stuck up on one side. Around his waist Bernie wore a tightly fitted rubber ring, which had the head of a prissy-faced unicorn at the front, and on both of his bony biceps were blown-up orange armbands that glowed in the sun. In spite of these childish trimmings, he looked to be about the same age as Beryl – with a wrinkled forehead, crumpled neck, and eyes which looked out from under two wild eyebrows thick like hairy caterpillars.

Baby-faced, Bernie was not.

'So you're the one hoping to take on my mantle? Mother has told me all about you,' he sneered. 'Fancy yourself a swimming prodigy, do you? The kid who almost drowned after less than three minutes in the water.'

Bernie's sing-song voice was surprisingly sharp. His vulture-like mother sat nearby on her scooter, a few paces down the dunes. She laughed with a bark that sounded like hard gravel crunching underfoot.

'That was only a test run,' Casper blushed. Beryl and Wynn appeared beside him on the deck of *Les Moules-Frites*, having followed the noise. 'I'm a brilliant swimmer, and you can bet that I'll be ready when the day comes.'

'And what day might that be?' gloated Bernie, pulling an oversized lollipop from somewhere beneath his inflatable unicorn. 'You've booked your crossing with the Channel Swimming Syndicate, have you? Oh, wait. I spoke to them this morning and there's not a soul under the age of seventy set to swim the Channel this summer.' He allowed himself one short, hearty laugh before he shoved the multi-coloured lollipop into his mouth.

'I'll talk to them,' Casper panicked. 'They'll understand once I tell them I don't have long left to break your record . . . They'll want to help.'

'And have your death on their conscience? I don't imagine that would be the best look for the organization.'

Casper could feel his dream slipping between his toes like melted ice cream, as if there were no webbings at all. Tears burned his eyes.

'Enjoy making young boys feel bad, do you, Bernie?' said Beryl, standing at Casper's side. Her hands clenched the tugboat's railing. 'When was the last time that you had a dream? The only challenge you've even dared take on was close to sixty-five years ago.'

'And what of it, Bazooka?' spluttered Bernie, the enormous lollipop glued to his swollen tongue. 'I still hold that record. I've nothing to prove to the likes of you.' He reached inside the neck of his swimming costume and pulled out a large gold medal which hung on an emerald ribbon. Bernie held the disc in the sunlight and Casper recognized the handsome merman engraved upon its face. It was the logo of the Channel Swimming Syndicate, and Bernie's reward for swimming the Channel.

'Records are made to be broken,' said Wynn, glaring down at Bernie. 'If Casper says he can swim the Channel, then I believe in him. You should probably start taking him seriously, because your time is over!'

Casper's heart swelled with warmth at the show of support from his new friend.

Bernie huffed, looking back to Casper. 'You'll never do it. No one has come *close* to breaking my record in six decades.' He looked to his mother with a curt nod. Agatha's glare moved slowly between each of the faces on board *Les Moules-Frites* with silent contempt.

She lingered on Casper.

'Oh, I'll break it,' he promised, eyeing the gold

medal resting on Bernie's chest. 'I may not have as much experience as you'd like, but I have a secret weapon and you'll be sorry.' He felt his rubbery feet tingle at the promise. They were itching to kick off Casper's clumpy shoes for good, so that he could dive into the ocean and never leave.

'Secret weapon? Don't make me laugh,' teased Bernie, even though he looked like laughter was the last thing on his mind. 'What trick could you possibly have up your sleeve to bring you *near* besting my record in time?'

'Me,' said Beryl calmly.

Casper, Wynn, Bernie and his mother all turned their heads in one joint motion.

'You?' asked Bernie. His long eyebrows waved furiously in the breeze as if to make their own silent protest.

'Me,' Beryl confirmed. 'I'm Casper's new swimmin' coach.'

'You are?' The boy with the webbed feet gasped. Casper's body overflowed with joy. It was more than he could have hoped for.

'I am.' Beryl glowered at Bernie. 'And I can't wait to see sixty years of arrogance wiped from your face once Casper lands on the beach at Cap Gris-Nez.'

'Like I said,' continued Bernie. 'There are no slots left. If he wants his swim to be recognized officially, then he's *too late*. Oh dear. What a shame!'

Casper felt Beryl's arm wrap around his shoulder, and expected to be led back inside with a squeeze. Instead, she stood firm and looked down at Bernie with resolve.

'He can have my spot,' she said.

'He can *what*?' cried Bernie, spitting sugary saliva across the sand in a rainbow of colour as he choked on both his anger and the lollipop.

'I'm booked for the end of August. I'd planned on breaking my own record again, because why not?' smiled Beryl, betraying a glimmer of enjoyment at Bernie's horror. 'It's like Wynn said . . . Records are made to be broken. Now, Casper can use my slot to break *yours*.'

Bernie's limbs shook with rage, softened only by the squeaking of the plastic armbands that rubbed his wrinkly skin. 'Well—' he stuttered. 'In that case, I'll enjoy the double satisfaction of watching you *both* fail!'

He turned and sloped his way back down the dunes, heading for the short row of beach huts in the distance.

His mother, Agatha, continued to stare at the trio on board *Les Moules-Frites*. Her eyes were alive with interest in spite of the stillness of her body. Her wraith-like hair wobbled in the wind while she took in the group. Her attention stayed fixed on Casper for a moment too long, until her eyes passed down the boy's legs and settled upon his clumpy black shoes.

Casper felt a cold chill run through his body. It travelled to the tip of his webbed toes, hidden behind their ungainly leather shields. A sickening feeling settled there, and he wriggled his feet as if to shake the anxiety loose.

Agatha couldn't possibly know his secret . . .

Casper had barely been in town for two days. Only Beryl had been in the water with him, and she hadn't noticed the webbing which stretched between his toes like a French accordion.

Finally, Agatha turned her scooter and drove back down to the beach, following her son like a lion stalking prey.

'Well,' said Wynn, breaking the tension. 'Those two are a total nightmare.'

'Nothing we can't handle,' promised Beryl. 'Just don't let them get to you. As for your Channel swim,' she said to Casper, suddenly serious, 'it will be the end of August before you've said the word "unicorn". You wanted my help and now you've got it, though you may yet live to regret it. If you're doing this, then you're doing it right.'

'I'm ready,' vowed Casper, excitement overflowing.

'I'll be setting you on the strictest regime imaginable,' said Beryl, tutting as she looked him up and down. 'You're a scrawny thing. What do you eat for breakfast?'

'Umm, at home its usually some kind of vegetable juice . . . But this morning Granny gave me a croissant and a plate of prunes.' He silently retched at the memory.

'Useless!' cried Beryl. 'I want you eating an adult's portion of pasta every morning without fail. We have to sort out that barnet of yours too,' she said, eyeing Casper's untamed and unkempt hair.

'What's wrong with my barnet?' he said.

'It's not exactly aerodynamic,' explained Beryl. 'Even with a swimming cap!'

'You don't want a scalping like Jeremy Jones, do you?' asked Wynn.

'Umm, no?' gulped Casper.

'Then a buzz cut it is!' Beryl declared. 'If you want to wipe that look off Bernie's face then we can't leave *anything* to chance. Meet me beneath the castle tomorrow morning at eight o'clock sharp, and we'll see to that haircut. But first, make sure you get a bowl of pasta in your belly after an ice-cold shower.'

'What?' said Casper, horrified. After years of washing in thunderstorms and torrential downpours, he'd only just discovered the joy of a bathtub filled with warm water.

'Do you want to have another near-drowning? We've got to get you used to the temperature, and quick. It's strictly cold showers from now on.'

'I've never been more grateful for a wetsuit,' laughed Wynn.

Casper ignored her. 'Can't we start training right now? I've got my trunks on.'

'Take this evening off,' said Beryl. 'In a few days' time you'll be wishing that you had never laid eyes on the English Channel, or ever even heard the name of Beryl the Bazooka.'

CHAPTER TWELVE

The Coral Room

Casper wandered up the woodland path in a daze. Finally, someone was willing to help him achieve his dream . . . He was going to swim the English Channel, and break Bernie's record in the process.

Baby Face Bernie was nothing like Casper had imagined. He had dined out on his childhood achievement from the moment he'd landed in France and even now, he seemed fixated on nothing but the glory of his record-setting swim.

Would the same be said of Casper in sixty years' time?

Beryl and Wynn had said that records were made to be broken. When a sprightly young person came along in the future and attempted to break Casper's own record, would he encourage the competition? Or would he become just as bitter as old Bernie?

Casper was still pondering this question as he sat at Ida's kitchen table eating dinner – a suspicious feast of corned beef and mashed potato.

'What's on your mind?' she asked, watching Casper push his food around the plate, lost in thought. 'You've barely touched your pea puree!'

The green foam bubbled on the china plate, and Casper held back a small gag.

'Nothing really,' he sighed.

'You can talk to me,' Ida promised. 'I want us to be really good friends. I promise, I'll listen to whatever's troubling you.'

'Well,' Casper said at last. 'I met Bernie Baxter today.' He wrinkled his nose with displeasure, picturing himself in the same swimming costume and armbands that Bernie had been sporting. Was that Casper's future?

'Oh,' smirked Ida. 'Well, then, I can certainly see why you might be feeling down.' She laughed, before her smile evaporated at the sight of Casper's frown.

'He was *nothing* like I'd thought . . . In every picture I've seen he seemed so happy, and he had such a kind face. Today he was mean and rude. And old!'

'Watch it!' teased Ida. 'He's younger than me, I'll have you know.'

'But "Baby Face"?' Casper laughed. 'Come off it.'

'He was certainly fresh in his swimming days. He was so young when he swam the Channel – it really was quite the achievement. But his mother, Agatha – well, she treated Bernie like a little hero.' Ida froze, quickly realizing the direction in which she had unconsciously taken the conversation.

Casper imagined the stout boy from the black-and-white photos being carried along the seafront on a litter, lined in red velvet and piled high with plump tasselled cushions. Bernie was being fed fat purple grapes by his mother, while tall men fanned him with palm leaves and swarms of people cheered.

'Anyway,' Ida recovered. 'Plenty of people have accomplished things which are just as remarkable.'

'Like Beryl!' smiled Casper.

'Um, yes. Like Beryl.'

'I think Dev's right – there's something special in the water here. Everyone has so much energy, it's like the town brings people back to life. I love it.'

'I'm glad you like Corallium, Casper,' Ida beamed, in spite of herself. 'But this is just a town. A beautiful one, for sure, but a town, nonetheless. There's nothing magical running through the pipes, and no secrets hidden in the soil. Corallium Castle is made of plain old stone just like this house.'

'How can you say that?' asked Casper. 'Dev says the castle might be coral, and this house? It's so strange. When I first arrived I could swear I saw the white sails of a ship soaring high above the roof. It was like I was standing on the sea floor, looking up towards the surface. And this morning—'

'Your imagination is running wild,' Ida said firmly. 'They're just stories, Casper.'

'I'm not so sure. I didn't even know about the legend before I met Wynn, though come to think of it, my coach driver could feel that there was something special here too. Pensioners are swimming the Channel or running up and down the cliffs like teenagers. There was even someone in the sea at dawn this morning . . .

'And you can't tell me that you don't feel that way too. It's like I was always meant to find my way here. Corallium has been waiting for me, all my life.'

'It's easy to believe that you've fallen under some kind of spell,' began Ida, stony-faced. 'This is a beautiful town, but you mustn't get swept away in a fantasy.'

'It's not even just about Corallium. I've felt this way for as long as I've known water. It's like the sea is pulling on my bones and I think it's all connected. There has to be a reason why I'm so at home here.'

'I want this to be like home, Casper.'

'But why do you bother staying here if you don't feel the same?' he asked. 'Why do you still have a beach hut when you think the sea is just a big wet waste of time?'

Ida had turned a shade of white to match her mashed potato. 'Casper—'

'I know there's something going on. It's like I'm a jigsaw puzzle and this town holds the missing piece.

You promised that I could tell you anything, so why won't you do the same?'

'Because I'm the adult, Casper,' Ida barked, quickly finding the limit to her patience. 'I've lived in Corallium my entire life, and it will always be home. Whether I enjoy the sea or not has no bearing on—'

'What?' Casper interrupted. 'You've lived here your entire life? Then, my dad was born here too. Did he grow up here?'

Ida stood, ignoring the question as she began to clear the plates from the table – their half-eaten dinner still warm. She tossed the china in the sink with a crash, and the sound of water rushing from the tap made Casper's throat feel dry.

'How can my dad have never told me this? He hates the water, even more than you do.' Casper thought back to his conversation with Beryl. 'The sea flows through my *soul*. I must have got that from somewhere ... From *someone*.'

Ida's face was screwed up in pain. 'I've said too much, Casper.'

'But I feel so different here. I feel *normal*, for the first time in my life. I belong here, and there must be a reason why I'd never even seen the sea until—' He stopped short, his recurring dreams quickly stirring in his mind's eye.

A baby-sized pair of webbed feet, splashing happily in the surf.

'I *have* been here before, haven't I?'

'Enough,' Ida shouted above the noise of the gushing tap, almost smashing the plate in her hand which she scrubbed with a wire scouring pad. 'This is the first time I've seen you since you were young, and that's only because your parents don't have a single working limb between them. It's not my place to tell you these things, or it'll be another ten years before you're allowed to come back. Your parents have their reasons for wanting to keep you away from Corallium, and from me.'

Casper felt an ache of longing run down his legs and through his feet like an electric current. 'You know what the sea means to me. You know that my parents have done everything they can to keep me on dry land. I have to understand *why* I feel like this.'

Ida released a long sigh.

For a second it seemed like she no longer had the energy to disagree, and would instead allow the truth to pour from her lips like the running water still spilling from the kitchen tap.

'I'm sorry,' she said sternly. 'The conversation is over.'

Casper pushed his chair from the table with a loud scrape and fled the room, rushing up the stairs two at a time. Angry thoughts ran through his head as he passed the locked hallway cupboard and the rows of picture-frame marks that stained the walls. He skidded to a halt outside the sitting room with a thump as a realization dawned. Not only did the dark markings continue across the walls inside, but for the first time he noticed that the room had no decorations of any kind. There were no ornaments or paintings, no little trinkets brought back from holidays of years gone by...

How could someone live in such a stark and sterile home? The strange house was just as cold inside as its stony exterior promised.

Unless...

Ida might have hidden her worldly possessions away in a last-minute dash through the building, just before Casper's sudden arrival. But why? Her pearl necklace, sleek hair and expensive trench coat betrayed a love for pretty things. This was *not* the home of someone as stylish and warm as his new granny. So where had everything gone?

The locked closet.

Casper tiptoed along the hallway and peered down towards the ground floor, when his stomach lurched at the memory of the phantom whirlpool. Recovering, he watched Ida appear from the kitchen and place a large shoe on the bottom stair before she paused, as if considering whether or not to take the first step. Casper rolled backwards into a silent heap.

Instead, Ida turned and wandered sadly into the kitchen.

'Phew,' he sighed with relief, realizing as he did that he'd been holding his breath for the last few seconds. Silently, Casper crept along the landing towards the cupboard and took the door handle in both hands. He gave it a hard shake in both directions.

Still locked.

He jiggled the door back and forth, hoping that it might somehow open from his sheer force of will, but there was no luck with that approach either. He knelt on the carpet, cringing as a floorboard groaned loudly under the weight of his knee like a snore escaping from the wood's restless slumber. There was still no movement from downstairs, so Casper risked placing one eye against the keyhole . . .

A strong smell of seawater found his nose, and he gasped.

Deep within the gloom of the cupboard he saw a flash of colour. A glimmer of pink, which slowly broke through the darkness with a hum like fire as Casper's eyes focused on the shape forming inside.

Sea coral!

Blush-coloured coils twisted up from the floor and wound their way around the narrow walls of the room, like a forest of creeping vines searching for sky.

Casper felt a soft nose against his leg and pulled away to find Triton by his side. The dog settled on the carpet beside him and gave a kindly yap.

'What's going on, boy?' Casper asked him quietly. 'How can this be possible?'

He hurried to look back through the keyhole but this time, to his disappointment, found only darkness. The coral was gone – as if whatever force was calling out had died of sudden exhaustion. Was it just another trick of the light, or tiredness, like the billowing sails and the flooded hallway floor?

But this was the *third* impossible thing he'd seen in Granny Ida's home.

Casper fell back on his hands. 'There's something going on inside this house, Triton. I know it. It feels like everyone in Corallium is keeping secrets...'

Triton gave another small yap of agreement and scurried down the carpet to sit by Casper's webbed feet, which were concealed inside the thickest pair of socks he owned. The dog gave them a knowing sniff.

'Even me,' acknowledged Casper.

CHAPTER THIRTEEN

Bernie's Nightcap

*B*aby Face Bernie sat at the kitchen counter, staring at the microwave while he waited patiently for it to ping.

Despite his confrontation with Beryl and her new band of sycophantic followers, Bernie was in a good mood. He was wearing his favourite pair of pyjamas, fresh from the tumble dryer – a bright red cotton set with a matching eye mask held in place by a thin elastic strap. The large superhero logo on his chest was partially hidden by the hefty gold medal, which Bernie wore around his neck even now.

PING!

He jumped up from the counter and ran to the microwave, pulling open the door to find his mug of milk frothing gently, to match his fizzing white eyebrows.

'Perfect,' he smiled, taking the scalding hot drink in his hands and slurping a large mouthful. A sickly film of milk skin stuck to his upper lip like a soggy handlebar moustache.

His mother came into the room on her scooter, a look of pure disdain on her face at the sight of her son's indulgence. Her fragile white hair was held on top of her head by a single plastic curler, and her body was swathed in a green silk nightgown that was dirty from the wheels of her ride. She picked out a fat prune from the large paper bag on her lap and tore it with her teeth.

'Ooh, can I have one?' asked Bernie, eyeing up the purple fruit.

'Keep your greasy mitts off,' barked Agatha, her gravelly voice as rough as a piece of sandpaper scrubbed against the hull of *Les Moules-Frites*. 'These prunes are good for my digestion. Youngsters like *you* don't need the help!'

'But, Mother—'

'What are you doing?' she asked accusingly.

'I'm having my bedtime drink,' Bernie whispered serenely. He peeled the milk moustache from his face and dropped it into his mouth with a satisfied smack of his lips. For Bernie, there was no greater pleasure.

'Bedtime?' his mother snapped. 'How can you even think about sleeping at a time like this . . . After a day like today!'

'Mother, it's late. Can't I relax? That Casper clown will have drowned by next week, either from incompetence or the curse,' chuckled Bernie. He continued to guzzle milk like a newborn calf, the liquid gently warming his throat on its journey to his stomach where it settled with a comforting glow.

The years had quickly crept up on Bernie 'Baby Face' Baxter, despite his youthful nickname. He was finally feeling his age and had grown to cherish these late-night moments of solitude, with a mug of milk and a warm pair of jammies. He looked up to the oven door and viewed his reflection while scratching his itchy head – the absurdly blonde hair, which framed his face like a tangle of dry yellow noodles; the deep crow's feet that stretched from behind his masked eyes and across his face like the map of a lifetime.

'You are too laid-back about these things,' scoffed Agatha, a mocking tone to her voice which Bernie had long grown accustomed to. His mother's teeth were black with sticky prune juice as she sneered. 'Do you really believe your record so unbreakable that Casper Delmare poses no threat?'

'Yes!' Bernie smiled. He scratched his scrawny belly with a sharp nail, the pale flesh peeking out from below his too-small pyjama top. He noticed a long hair growing from his belly button like a white wire and plucked it, holding it up to the light with interest. 'That Delmare boy has barely a scrap of spare flesh on his bones. When I swam the Channel—'

Agatha's eyes grew misty. 'When you swam the Channel you were the perfect picture of a champion! A stocky young swimming sensation with the world at his feet. You proved everybody wrong, and I was the proudest mother on Earth that day . . .'

Bernie glowed, his red pyjama top a fraction darker than his flushed face.

'But look at you now,' Agatha said, her expression darkening. 'What else have you done to make me proud in the last sixty years?'

'What more would you have had me do?' he asked, offended. 'No one has ever forgotten the name of Bernie "Baby Face" Baxter. It will go down in history! I achieved something on that day that no one else has managed since.'

'Yes,' said Agatha with a knowing frown. 'But you underestimate this boy. He has a drive unrivalled by any child I've seen, since . . . Irene Ingleby.'

'Irene?' babbled Bernie. His face was alive with shock, his eyebrows so high that they disappeared in his mess of blonde curls.

Agatha drove her scooter from the kitchen in silence and Bernie followed, the mug of milk still warming his bony hands like a hot-water bottle.

They came to a stop in the lounge, a stifling room littered with itchy woollen blankets, cushions and an unpleasant rug made from the hide of an alligator. The focal point was a feature wall painted olive green. It shimmered with a dozen picture frames of gold and silver, which hung like ornate jewels above a roaring fireplace.

Each frame held a photo of Bernie.

But rather than a rogues' gallery depicting a person's long and happy life, every single frame displayed a snap of the same cherub-like boy in an old-fashioned swimming costume. A young Bernie was pictured stepping into the shallow waters of Corallium; swimming in the wide-open sea while enormous freight ships passed by in the background; and standing on the rocks outside France with a thumb held high in the air. The wall was an opulent shrine to one single day in the long life of the elderly man known as Baby Face Bernie.

'Look at these photos,' said Agatha, motioning to the wall with a lazy wave of one arm. 'You might be *someone* right now, but you can bet your bottom that your name will be nothing if that boy makes the crossing. You'll be scrubbed from the history books, and Casper Delmare will be the newest toast of the town.'

'But how can you possibly think he'll make it?' insisted Bernie. He slumped into a chintzy armchair beside the sooty black fireplace, placing his milk on the table. 'That boy went into the sea for the first time in his whole life yesterday, and he almost drowned!'

'He *would* have drowned if it weren't for the Bazooka. She was in that water faster than you get through a tube of Trésor de la Mer.'

Bernie dolefully picked a piece of flaking skin from his knee. 'Flipping expensive stuff.'

'There's something about that boy,' continued Agatha, chewing an especially large prune. 'I can't quite put my finger on what – but he *really* wants that record. He's determined, I'll give him that. It feels dangerous . . .'

A loud crunch came from inside Agatha's mouth. She winced in irritation and spat a large stone from the purple fruit between her teeth directly into the fireplace. It landed among the flames like a bullet, the orange blaze roaring as the stone sizzled loudly on the burning logs.

'. . . and I *don't* like it.'

'Well, what do you want me to do?' sighed Bernie, attempting to muster the energy needed for whatever ludicrous task his mother was about to set. She threw a black swimming costume, cap and matching snorkel into his lap.

'You can't be serious?' he said with a gasp.

'Deadly.' Prune juice dripped down Agatha's chin

while her purple eyes reflected the fireplace, which danced across her face with the promise of violence.

Bernie scratched his blonde head, relieving the rash on his scalp which would flare up like an old enemy when his mother delegated dubious work. He was often in awe of his ancient old mum; she held a darkness that could chill him to the bone.

You don't live to be one hundred and five without making some enemies, he thought, pushing down the stray voice which frequently told him that Agatha Baxter was not a kind woman. She had always been kind to *him*.

Hadn't she?

'Now get those superhero jammies off and get to work,' she hissed.

Agatha gave her son one last look of disdain and turned her scooter, driving from the room with an ominous hum. Bernie was left alone in front of the dying fireplace, his long shadow stretching low across the crocodile rug like the twisted trunk of a knotted tree. He picked up his milk, feeling through the mug that it had already gone cold.

'Goodnight, then, Mother,' he said to the empty room.

If this is what it took to make her proud, then of course he would do it.

What other choice did he have?

CHAPTER FOURTEEN

A Blue Rinse and a Buzz Cut

The following morning, Casper sat in Ida's kitchen with a plate piled high with pasta. It felt like an odd choice for breakfast, but who was he to question the methods of Beryl the Bazooka? After eating as much as he could – which wasn't a lot, seeing as his stomach hadn't woken up yet – he scooped the leftovers into a container and jumped from the table.

'Why does it smell like a bad Italian bistro?' asked Ida groggily, appearing at the bottom of the stairs with Triton. 'And why are you up so early?'

'I said I'd meet Wynn. She wants me to watch her surf.' Casper felt bad for the rubbish lie, but he'd spent half the night in bed trying to think of a good reason to sneak away and meet Beryl.

Triton ran to his side and greeted his hand with a wet lick.

'All right,' replied Ida, yawning. 'Well, have a nice day. I suppose I'll see you for lunch?'

'Probably not before tonight, it's going to be a long one. After, we might go and see what her dad's been excavating. Apparently there's some pretty cool stuff.'

'Ah.'

Casper twiddled his thumbs awkwardly. 'I'm sorry about all the pans in the sink, I had a really strong craving for spaghetti...'

'I see,' said Ida, bewildered.

'And I probably will every morning from now on—' said Casper, halfway out of the door. 'OK, thanks, bye!' He threw the words as quickly as he could, charging from the house and up the cobbled streets before he could be questioned any further.

'Have a nice day!' Ida called from the doorstep.

Guilt pummelled Casper's insides, as if his stodgy breakfast had formed an angry fist that pounded his stomach. He didn't want to keep secrets from Ida, but he was frustrated too. There was something important that she wasn't telling him ...

And Casper needed to swim.

Now that he'd found his way to Corallium, nothing was ever going to stand in the way of that again.

When Casper reached the village green, he stared up at the craggy castle in awe. Its barnacle-like lumps and knotted spires were such a peculiar sight on dry land.

Could the legends really be true?

Casper had never believed in magic. Neptune or Poseidon, mermaids, sirens, selkies and whatever other mythical creatures might have once called this land their underwater kingdom were just that – *myths*. In school he'd learnt that some of the world's highest mountains were still growing by a few centimetres every year. But that was a *glacial* pace! It would take hundreds of thousands of years for the earth to shift so much that the cliffs of Corallium, the woodland walk and even the coral castle would be pushed up through the waves.

It was impossible, surely, but then again—

'Casper!'

He turned to see Beryl striding down the street towards him with purpose. Her pink hair was glistening with water, no doubt from an early morning swim.

Casper's feet shivered with envy.

'I'm glad you're up,' she said, surveying Casper's shaggy blonde mane which covered one eye completely. 'This could take even longer than I'd imagined.'

Casper gave the castle one last look before following Beryl down one of the skeletal streets, which ran from the green like winding rivers of stone. The ground felt especially bumpy, and he looked down to find the hollows of enormous moon shells, conches and giant clams hammered into the pavement.

They passed the neon sign of the bingo hall which spluttered half-heartedly, exhausted from whatever had taken place inside its walls the previous evening. Casper smiled as he imagined Dev fighting off a group of pensioners for a new electric toothbrush.

'Hustle, ladies!' he heard a voice call from behind.

It was the same group of women Casper had seen at the funicular station the previous day. They zipped around the castle in single file, running at full speed like a chundering train carriage topped with white hair. Each woman wore the same floral tracksuit, with lacy collar and matching filigree cuffs, along with a pair of slick sunglasses that reflected the morning sun in fluorescent purple lenses. They moved like an elderly army, breathing in time with the beat of their bouncy rubber trainers which sprung from the fossilized cobbles.

'Three more laps around the castle, then we're on to the bikes!' cheered their leader, who Casper remembered was called Mabel. 'Push through the pain, ladies, push!'

He watched the group disappear around another bend and whistled in awe.

'Here we are, then,' declared Beryl, bringing Casper back to attention. The pair had stopped outside a souvenir shop whose windows were packed with glass vials filled with Corallium seawater, and small pieces of 'genuine' coral chipped from the castle.

'What has this got to do with training?' asked Casper.

'No, not that shop full of old toot—'

'HEY!' came the angry voice of a shopkeeper inside.

'*Here*,' said Beryl. She pointed to the dusty hair salon next door, and Casper frowned at the pictures on display in the window. Headshots of elderly women covered the glass and every single one stared back with the very same coiffed blue curls as the last.

'Are you sure about this?' asked Casper. 'It doesn't look like they even do short hair, let alone kids.'

Beryl ushered him through the door. 'Don't be daft. They've had no kids to practise on before now, have they?'

Despite the early hour, the salon was open with two women visible inside. One stood mopping the teal green tiled floor, which was already unnaturally clean. The other sat reading a magazine while her head buzzed loudly from inside an enormous, helmet-like hair dryer. Along the walls on either side of the room were large art deco mirrors shaped like rays of sunshine, and in front of each was a bizarre chair shaped like an open oyster shell. Every seat had a long metal tongue which rolled down to the floor where it formed a pearl-like footrest.

Casper looked up to the ceiling. It was decorated with an extravagant but worn tile mosaic, which seemed to depict the underwater version of Corallium he'd been hearing about. Shoals of fish swam through the streets and around the castle in a ribbon of faded colour. At the centre, a muscular merman held a gold trident above his head, which was missing – his face having been stolen from the ceiling by gravity.

'Beryl!' yelped the woman cleaning the floor, when she noticed them standing in the doorway. She dabbed her forehead with the end of the mop. 'Surely you don't need another cut already? And your colour . . . It's positively luminous!'

'Sheila!' cheered Beryl. She performed an exaggerated twirl and zhuzhed the side of her pink head with one hand. 'No, I'm here this morning with my young friend, Casper.' Beryl shunted him forward, pushing him into one of the armchairs which was surprisingly comfy, despite its cumbersome shape.

'The boy?' started Sheila, her voice laced with horror. 'I don't know, Beryl. I've not done a boy's hair since . . . ever, actually.'

'I think you'll find that boys' hair and girls' hair, and everyone else's hair for that matter, grows in a very similar fashion.'

'Well, all right,' Sheila muttered. 'If you say so – but no refunds, and no funny business! I'll just go and get the curling iron warmed up—'

'What?' cried Casper, picturing his own permed head in place of one of the shopfront's pampered models. He tried to wriggle out from the seat, but was held in place by Beryl's tight grip on his shoulder.

'No need for that, Sheila. We're just giving Casper a nice clean buzz cut.'

'Oh, no, not him as well,' groaned Sheila. 'You mean, just short? The same length all over, like your sides?'

'That's right,' smiled Beryl. 'Lop it all off, *phwip*!' She mimed cutting through Casper's messy barnet with the palm of her hand as though it were a sharpened axe.

'But it's just so inflexible! A buzz cut leaves no room for an artist, such as I, to express myself. Though I suppose we could add some personality with a blue rinse—'

'No. Blue. Rinse,' protested Casper loudly.

'But that's my speciality!' said Sheila, the disappointment dripping audibly from her tongue. She folded her arms in a sulk.

'We just need to make Casper a little more aerodynamic,' instructed Beryl. 'He'll be swimming the Channel at the end of August, an' every little helps.'

'Will he indeed?' sighed Sheila. Casper assumed that her lack of enthusiasm was a symptom of life in Corallium. Living in a town where elderly women regularly completed a triathlon on a Monday morning must take the shine off physical achievement . . .

Sheila unwrapped a large cape and draped it loosely over Casper's head, engulfing him in itchy polyester. After a moment's pause, in which the salon owner stood staring at him uncertainly, she began to ruffle his hair with her fingers.

'Right,' she said. 'We could just . . . No, that'll never . . . Or how about . . . Oh, that won't work—'

'For goodness' sake,' interrupted Beryl. She pulled a trolley of hair equipment across the room and began to rummage through it, finally finding a box in one of the lower drawers which still had a paper price tag swinging from its corner. Beryl tore the box open, pulled out an electric shaver and blew the remnants of her own pink hair from the blades. She held it out to Sheila.

'How old are you, anyway?' the hairstylist asked Casper, one eyebrow raised.

'I'll be twelve soon.'

'But that means you'd break Bernie's record! Oh, no.' Sheila backed away from the mirror with her hands held up. 'I don't want any part in this. Beryl, you should be ashamed – you know very well what happens every time a child tries this.'

'You mean the "curse"?' asked Casper, his skin prickling despite his scepticism.

'Don't!' gasped Sheila. 'Don't even say the word. I'll not have you bringing bad luck on my head too. If you want to risk your life, that's your business, but leave me out.'

'Fine, I'll do it myself!' declared Beryl, changing the setting to grade one and clicking the shaver's power button.

The razor touched the back of Casper's skull and sent a ripple of vibrations through his body. It felt as if he'd rested his head on the window of a moving train, the tremors travelling across his skin with a strange wave-like buzz.

'How does that length feel?' Beryl asked above the noise.

Casper looked up to the mirror and studied his reflection. Long strands of thick blonde hair continued to fall past his eyes like bushy bales of hay, landing on his lap in a messy pile of clippings. Although one half of his head was still covered in scruffy hair, the other side felt positively buoyant. A breeze from the open door blew through the shop to tickle his exposed scalp with a pleasant shiver, which felt as cool as the ocean running across his webbed feet.

'It's brilliant,' he grinned.

Sheila dabbed her forehead, at a loss for what to do with herself. She picked up a plastic tray and began to mix blue hair dye, just to keep busy.

A short while later, Casper's head felt light as a feather.

'A few more patches and we're . . . almost . . . done,' said Beryl, her tongue between her teeth while she concentrated. 'There!'

Casper stared into the mirror.

If it weren't for the familiar smile stretched across

his face, he might've questioned who the strange boy looking back at him was. It was as if he'd shed a layer of skin, alongside the pile of golden hair now knotted by his knees.

It felt exposing too. He hadn't quite realized just how much his shaggy locks had been like a shield – something to hide behind when he didn't want the boys at school to bother him, or when his parents launched into a webby rant at home . . . Now, there was nothing left to defend him.

Casper felt dangerous, and powerful.

He felt more ready than ever.

CHAPTER FIFTEEN

The Proper Technique

'Keep your bum in the air!' shouted Beryl. She was treading water, up to her neck in the sea beside Casper who struggled to keep his legs on the surface. The sun beat down, and Beryl's luminous hair shone brightly like a hot-pink bonfire as her head bobbed on the waves.

Casper lifted his face from the water. 'How am I supposed to keep my bum in the air when all it wants to do is sink?'

'By learning the proper technique!'

'I've managed fine swimming my way all this time,' continued Casper, wheezing. 'I swam for more than eight hours once, with no rest, and I've never been this tired in my life!'

'You wouldn't *be* so out of breath if you were *breathin'* effectively,' Beryl countered. 'This isn't your neighbour's minnow pond now, kid. You won't find any loose change at the bottom of the Channel, but you will land yourself in real trouble – *if* you aren't prepared.'

Casper huffed.

Beryl wouldn't be this hard on him if she knew about his webbed feet. None of the other children who'd tried to break the 'curse' of the Channel record had such an incredible advantage. His flippers were proof that Casper had been born for swimming. Maybe he should tell her the truth and be done with it? His parents had always overreacted . . .

'Beryl,' he started. The words edged their way around his tongue until a vision of his parents' disapproving faces wobbled in his mind.

'Never mind,' he finished, after a pause. He couldn't

risk it. Casper loved his feet, but what if Beryl thought he was a freak like his parents promised?

'Well,' she said, shooting him a curious glance but allowing the moment to pass. 'Head down, eyes forward. If you can keep your stomach flat on the surface, then the rest of your body will want to do the same.'

Casper put his face back in the water, and through his goggles the sea was as clear as the water in Ida's bathtub. Even three metres down he could spy a crab on the seabed, which was a rippling desert of shimmering hills. A shoal of tiny silver fish swam past like one long sheet of silk, caught in the current. Casper felt more at home in the sea than anywhere he'd ever been before, and happier too.

'Are you listening?' tutted Beryl, sensing that Casper's mind was elsewhere.

'Sorry,' he gurgled.

'Starting with both of your arms stretched out in front, move the first one backwards in a three-sweep motion . . . That's what gives you your forward momentum,' instructed Beryl. Water lapped at Casper's ears, causing her voice to come in and out of his hearing. 'First you sweep the arm forward, then back towards your body an' finally out past your thigh – like an hourglass shape.'

Casper followed Beryl's instructions. He waved his arm gracefully down the side of his body and felt himself move forward – slowly, but smoothly. The water rolled across his newly shaven head with a cool and pleasant sensation.

'That's the ticket! Just make sure that the action is complete before your arm leaves the water at the end...'

Casper continued the one-sided stroke and Beryl's instructions slowly rose into a shout as he moved further away. He looked up to find her, but Beryl had already caught up – her own swimming stroke effortless, and powerful.

'Your entire shoulder should surface as you lift your arm from the water,' she continued without missing a beat. 'Keep the elbow slightly bent, then reach out in front of your body an' slice through the water like a knife. Your arm can join the other still stretched out ahead, ready for the next stroke.'

Casper was confused. He couldn't help thinking that swimming was a lot less complicated when he was left to follow his instincts. Swirling around the shallow supermarket fountain was so easy that Casper could count every single coin on the bottom with one breath.

But Beryl was right.

The sea was a different beast, and he would need to make sure that every last drop of energy was used effectively. It was the only way that he'd ever manage to swim the whole way to France.

He continued to listen to Beryl's instructions, following each one to the letter, and before long, he was gliding across the water faster than ever. Each arm cut through the waves like an oar, and he switched from one to the other without the slightest pause. After five strokes, he lifted his face to take a short breath but his legs, and bum, began to quickly sink towards the depths once again.

'Small turns, lad,' encouraged Beryl. 'If you lift your whole head, your body will keep sinking. Leave your face in the water an' turn it slightly to the side ... Stretch your mouth an' you should be able to take a breath while staying pretty much underwater.'

Casper put his face back down and tried the stroke again. After three motions he turned to the side and took a full breath through the corner of his mouth.

He was soaring through the waves like a wooden arrow leaving its bow.

'You've got it!' cheered Beryl. 'Now exhale under-water while you swim, ready for your next breath on the opposite side in a few strokes' time . . .'

Casper continued swimming and allowed the swell of the sea to dictate his movement while he grew attuned to the push and pull of the waves, which seemed to work with him in harmony. The bands of skin between his long toes unfurled, urging him forward even faster. His feet sang at the freedom.

'Brilliant!' said Beryl, having swum to his side. 'You'll be faster than me soon! Just make sure t'keep your legs together.' She reached out and grabbed his ankle.

'No!' Casper yelped. He quickly pulled his legs below the surface, causing him to tumble backwards in an underwater somersault. He surfaced, coughing as a large wave crashed against the back of his neck.

'Sorry, I didn't mean—' He stumbled on the words, the thought of concealing his webbed feet from Beryl the only thing on his mind. 'I just really hate people touching my feet, they're really ticklish.'

Beryl looked nonplussed. 'Casper, there's nothing I'd like to do less than touch your smelly, sweaty feet.

I was just saying that you need to keep your legs together. Even on the downward kick, you only want to bend them slightly at the knee.'

Casper tried again, and again, and finally managed to clear his mind of worry once Beryl had turned her attention elsewhere. His feet relaxed, and he was soaring through the water once more.

'That's brilliant,' Beryl cheered. 'With the Bazooka technique, and that sharp new buzz cut, you'll be near unstoppable!'

That, and my webbed feet, thought Casper.

A few hours later, Beryl and her star pupil emerged from the sea. Their skin was wrinkled like two old prunes, and a steady stream of salt water slipped down from their bodies to the beach. Wynn sat patiently on the sand with a bunch of yellow bananas and some bottled water.

'Casper, you looked great!' she cheered, handing them each a piece of fruit. 'Maybe you really are a swimmer.' She winked playfully.

'Ha ha, thanks,' Casper smiled. He quickly dug his webbed feet into the loose sand like spades, shielding the toes from view.

'Tea?' called Beryl from inside the beach hut.

Casper heard the rattle of a kettle on top of the hob. 'Yes, please,' he and Wynn said in unison.

'I need an extra mug. Casper, could you have a look in Ida's cupboard and see what you can find?' asked Beryl. 'They'll be filthy, but nothing a good blast of the tap won't sort.'

Casper shovelled his feet through the sand towards his grandmother's grimy, unloved beach hut and stopped. Tan was standing at the bottom of the woodland walk, lurking in the long purple heather and staring at the water. His expression was wistful, and Casper could feel the yearning which seemed to emanate from him like fuzzy waves of heat.

Tan turned and caught his eye. Casper waved, before the teenager scowled and fled into the darkness of the damp woodland.

Despite Tan's frostiness, Casper couldn't help feeling for him. Two years ago they might've found themselves the best of friends, but now it seemed Tan couldn't face coming closer to the water than the heather walk.

Would Casper feel the same if he failed *his* swim?

He turned back to Ida's beach hut and stepped inside – dripping seawater on the carpet with every step of his enormous sandy feet. He reached up to open the first cabinet and found a few sad items, including a wooden spade, a bucket and some moulds in the shape of shells and crabs. He turned his attention to the second cupboard, hovering high above Ida's own ancient stovetop.

He opened the stiff door with a clatter.

An assortment of dusty mugs sat beside an old copper kettle, which was tucked neatly inside behind a thick brown rope. Standing on his tiptoes, which made him unusually tall thanks to the length of his flippers, Casper reached up to grab one of the mugs when suddenly—

The rope moved.

He yelped in fright and fell backwards to the floor.

'What is it?' asked Wynn, appearing beside him in the grotty beach hut. She looked up to the open cupboard. 'It's a grass snake! There must be a hole at the back of the cupboard somewhere.'

'Aren't you scared?' asked Casper. His heart was racing from the shock of finding a real-life snake just a few centimetres from his outstretched fingertips.

'Grass snakes are practically harmless. It must have made a nest in your granny's cupboard! Let's leave it alone, but keep the doors open. That might encourage it to slither back out through the hole. Then we can seal it up.'

'Good idea,' replied Casper, his voice shaking as Wynn reached up to take a mug from the cupboard. The snake was already uncoiling itself and winding its way towards a small patch of green in the wall. Casper realized it was the woodland peeking through a hole, and that Wynn had been right.

'Not scared of a little old grass snake, are you, boy?'

Casper spun around, his wet trunks sticking to the mucky floor as he tried to stand up.

It was Bernie, *of course*.

Today he was dressed as a cowboy, his all-in-one polyester swimming costume printed to look like the distressed denim of a sheriff in the Wild West. A comically small Stetson hat sat on top of his blonde curls, and a plastic badge hung limply from his chest beside the fat golden medal which swung from the ribbon around his neck.

'You should be more careful,' Bernie sneered with mock concern, exposing several sharp yellow teeth. 'A bite from a snake might put you out of action . . . You'd be too poorly to keep up with your training, and we wouldn't want that. You've so little time left.'

His mother appeared on the sand behind and howled like a banshee. The sound of her laughter sent a tremor down Casper's spine.

'I love the haircut,' she whispered.

Her voice rattled like rusty chains, and it made Casper's blood run cold. She was still laughing as she drove her scooter along the beach towards the woodland path. Bernie pulled a brown inflatable horse up around his waist and galloped quickly after her.

'Forget them!' declared Wynn. She looked around the neglected beach hut with a wrinkled nose. 'This place is absolutely filthy.'

'I know,' replied Casper sadly. He looked down at the mug in Wynn's hands and gasped. It was just like Beryl's – emblazoned with the merman logo of the Channel Swimming Syndicate.

Why would Ida have one of these? he thought.

Casper shifted his wet feet about in the grime, thinking, when the dripping sound of water falling from his body drew his attention to the floor. He looked down and saw that the red pawprints, which Triton had left on their last visit, had been joined by the large shape of Casper's own wet bottom.

'Hold on,' he said, staring at the carpet. He moved his foot, still caked in sand, and found another damp mark in its place.

A deep, red footprint with flecks of yellow.

Casper bent over and shook his shaved head like a wet dog, watching as the dirt continued to melt away wherever the water landed. He brushed it with his hands. They were quickly covered in the grotty, wet mixture as more and more of the carpet was exposed.

'Gross,' said Wynn, turning from the cupboard where she had carefully closed up the snake's entrance hole with small rocks. 'Let's clean this place later with proper soap; your hands are disgusting!'

'No, look!' replied Casper, pointing to the rich colours of the carpet which had slowly been revealed through the water. A pattern of coral, in red and yellow, spread across the floor of the room. He remembered the photo in his bedroom back at Ida's home. Hadn't his dad been sitting on a red-and-yellow carpet just like this?

Casper closed his eyes, and the recurring dream of his baby feet splashing in the sea came back into view. The dreams which felt more like memories . . .

'I've been to Corallium before,' he whispered.

CHAPTER SIXTEEN

Pink and Gold

Casper ran back to Ida's house and, after scooping the picture frame from the windowsill in his room, lay on his bed and stared at the photo inside until dinner. There was no doubt that it was taken at the beach hut, right here in Corallium.

Casper had been here as a baby.

The dreams of water lapping his webbed toes weren't merely his imagination longing for the sea.

They were memories, which Casper had clung to subconsciously for all of these years . . . Something had caused his parents to leave Corallium, never to return or even mention that the town, or his grandmother, existed.

But what?

The framed photograph was Casper's first and only clue, but he knew there would be more – locked away inside Ida's secret cupboard. It was the only place in the whole house that his grandmother could have hidden the rest of her worldly possessions.

The clues to their family secret.

The cupboard's contents seemed to pulsate through the floorboards of the building, teasing Casper with the promise of answers. Since arriving in Corallium he'd been so preoccupied with swimming the Channel but now, even though he was closer than ever to achieving that dream, the thoughts were pushed from his mind by the image of a locked door and the tiniest glimmer of pink coral through a keyhole.

What didn't he know?

'Casper, what are you doing in the freezer?' asked Ida, entering the kitchen a couple of days later to find her grandson sitting inside one of the frosty drawers.

'I think I had too much sun today,' Casper fibbed, sandwiched between a bag of frozen peas and a container of unknowable beige mush. 'I thought this might help cool me down ...' Really, Beryl had ordered him to ramp up his cold-water training, adding a daily trip into the freezer to his arctic morning showers.

'Actually, Granny,' continued Casper, putting his new plan into action, 'I was wondering, would you tell me a little bit more about my dad?'

Ida's face fell. The two of them had only had the politest of awkward conversation for the last few days, meeting over Casper's daily breakfast of bolognese and again for dinner. Ida had acknowledged her grandson's newly shaven head with nothing more than a raised eyebrow.

'Not this again,' she said wearily. 'I told you, your parents have their reasons for keeping you away from Corallium, and I won't go against their wishes. Their secrets are not mine to share.'

'So they *do* have secrets!' declared Casper. He stood from the freezer drawer in triumph, lifting a bag of green beans which were stuck to his bottom with him.

Ida met him with silence, broken only by the icy bag which fell to the floor with a crunch. She folded herself into one of the kitchen chairs and put her hands on the table.

'I'm sorry,' said Casper, recovering. 'It's just – I've been looking at the photo you left on my windowsill. The one of my dad, with me as a baby. I'd never seen it before, and he looks so happy. I've never seen him like that, it's . . . really nice.'

He felt Ida soften. She was clearly pleased that her small gesture had interested him. Casper saw her hands relax and the colour return to her knuckles, which had been taut white.

'That's a lovely snap,' she said finally. 'Your parents sent me a copy when you were young . . . I think it was taken at their first house in Bramble-in-the-Oaks.'

The lie made Casper's pulse quicken. His webbed feet throbbed their disapproval as the blood pumped around his body like a log flume. 'We don't have a lot of photos at home; I'd love to see more.'

'I'm sure I have a few,' beamed Ida, relieved to have moved on from the topic of secrets. She stood from the table. 'Let me have a rummage and I'll see what I can find, while you . . . stay here.' She eyed Casper warily and backed out of the room, closing the door behind.

Once Casper was alone he listened intently to the muffled scrape of a wooden drawer open in the hallway, followed by the jangle of keys. After a pause, he heard Ida brush past the door and start to make her way up the staircase, each step creaking audibly under her feet. Slowly, Casper tiptoed towards the hall and pressed his ear against the door. He counted her steps.

Nine. Ten. Eleven.

He waited for Ida to reach the first landing, beyond certain of her destination without being able to see a single thing, and then—

The sound of a key in its lock, turning. A tiny click, the unmistakeable squeak of a cupboard door swinging open with an agonized groan. For the first time since Casper had arrived in Corallium, the mysterious hallway closet was open.

And now, Casper knew where Ida kept its key.

But he wanted to know, right now, what secrets were hidden inside the coral room. Hadn't he waited long enough for the truth? Casper grabbed the kitchen door handle and turned, peeling it open as smoothly as a ripened banana. He took a deep breath, tiptoed over to the bottom of the staircase and began the ascent one delicate step at a time – balancing the weight of his webbed feet evenly with each one placed at opposite ends of the beam.

Nine. Ten. Eleven.

He counted again, passing by the shadow-like stains of the picture frames which had once covered the walls. The back of Ida's curly hair rose into view. She was huddled over, rummaging through the cupboard which was open only a fraction – just enough to fit her face through the gap while she searched for photos.

Fourteen. Fifteen. Sixteen.

Casper reached the landing, craning his neck in a silent effort to see around Ida and glimpse the precious knowledge of the cupboard's contents, the smell of seawater finding his nostrils. Just as a flash of pink coral flickered in his vision, winking with a promise of the truth, Ida turned and screamed at the top of her lungs.

'Casper!' she panted, flustered by the scare. 'I told you to wait downstairs.'

'I know, but I thought I could help you look,' he fibbed. The temptation to rush past his grandmother and tear through the contents of the unlocked cupboard was overwhelming, but he managed to resist.

'I've found a few more photos,' she said. Ida pushed the cupboard door closed behind her with a bump of her bottom. 'Come to the sitting room and we'll look through them together . . . Oh, wait. Hold out your arms.'

She passed a pile of picture albums to Casper, took a long silver key from her pocket and locked the door behind her.

'Come along,' she said, leading a dutiful Casper down the first-floor landing. He felt the cupboard screaming at him with every step in the opposite direction, begging him to turn around and rip its door from the hinges.

Later that night Casper lay awake, waiting, and by two o'clock had grown too impatient. He threw off his duvet and crept across the room.

Silence rang through the building, while outside the gentle crash of the waves murmured softly. Casper briefly glanced out of the window into blackness, his curtains open on the white stars which twinkled down to the inky waves. They lapped tenderly at the shore's edge with a foamy kiss.

Then he saw them, and gasped.

Once again, a person was standing in the water – immobile, as still as the starlight, their long arms stretched wide as though to welcome the ocean in an embrace.

Triton had woken from Casper's yelp, and the dog trotted over to nestle his furry face in the boy's bare webbed feet.

'Who *is* that?' whispered Casper, picking the dog up in his arms. 'First they're standing in the sea before dawn, and now again at two in the morning!'

Triton turned towards the ocean, spotted the silhouette and barked.

'Quiet, boy!' Casper begged, placing him back on the floor. Triton put his paws on the wall and barked again, longing for a second look at the person he'd seen. 'You have to keep quiet, or you'll wake up Ida. Please!'

Luckily, Triton listened this time.

Casper held his breath, waiting for the noise of his grandmother stirring. The absence of sound felt louder than a scream, but there was no sign that Ida had woken.

When he looked out again at the darkened waves, the figure had disappeared.

Casper shook his head, at a loss. But there was only time to solve one mystery this evening . . .

'Wait here, boy,' he said to Triton, who had already flopped over on his side and given in to tiredness. 'I'll be back soon.'

Casper slipped into the hallway and peered over the banister, straining his eyes to see down through the building and on to each of the empty floors below.

Darkness.

He crept along the stairs as softly as a panther, down to the second floor and Ida's bedroom – which he tiptoed past at a positively glacial pace, his heart pounding with each step. Once he was safely out of range, he repeated the same silent strides while moving down the next staircase and across to the first-floor cupboard. It looked exactly as it had on his very first day in Corallium.

Except this time, Casper knew that it would open.

He placed a hand in his pyjama pocket and pulled out the long silver key, which he had pinched from the hallway drawer on his way to bed. He placed the key inside the lock and the mechanism clicked with a satisfying snap.

He grabbed the doorknob and pulled.

Inside it was pitch black – no sign of the teasing glimpse of pink coral. He moved his hands about in blindness, searching for a light cord, which he found and pulled with one firm tug. A dim light flickered to life above his head with a low buzz.

'Wow.'

The room was filled with coral, though not as he'd expected. An enormous painting, framed in gold and depicting Corallium Castle in stunning detail, stretched the width of the closet – which must've been the pink he'd seen through the keyhole. But . . . the coral garden had seemed so real! Hadn't Casper smelt salty seawater, and seen pink veins creeping up the wall? He tipped the painting on its side and found another large frame, this one holding an illustration of an ancient city – Corallium, under-water. The same image depicted on the hair salon's mosaic ceiling.

'Why would Granny keep this?' Casper wondered. 'She said that the legends were a load of nonsense for tourists . . .'

There were other frames too, stacked against the side of the cupboard like dominoes, and with a ripple of wonder Casper understood what had once hung along the walls of Ida's home: countless photos of Ida and Beryl, taken on adventures all across the country. In each, Beryl smiled to the camera with her hand firmly in Ida's. Their faces were a picture of happiness.

But why hide these? Was it Ida and Beryl's relationship that had kept his parents away for all these years? Were they *ashamed* of her? Surely they must've known about Beryl, and all this time while Casper had idolized her achievements from afar.

Why weren't they still together?

In the corner of one eye, a glint of gold caught Casper's attention. The framed illustration of Corallium had tipped forward to reveal a tall set of shelves, set against the back wall. An incredible collection of medals, trophies, plaques and goblets jostled for place amid a sea of shimmering metal. Each one was engraved with pictures of swimmers, ocean waves or octopus tentacles. Casper gasped when he saw that some had the words 'Ida Delmare' etched in the gold.

Beside the glossy awards were rosettes and ribbons of every colour of the rainbow, piled high along with certificates and more framed posters for swimming events and galas around the world.

All Casper had ever wanted to do was swim and here he was, by the sea for the first time in his life and having to sneak around in secret while his grandmother lied to him.

Ida didn't hate the ocean at all.

She was a *champion swimmer*.

CHAPTER SEVENTEEN

The Veins of Corallium

'I just don't get it,' Casper said to Wynn the following day. 'Why would Ida keep this a secret? She asked me to stay on dry land even though she knows how much I want to swim, and all this time she's been a champion swimmer!'

Beryl had given Casper the day off from training, not that it had stopped him craving a chilly morning dip. His short hair was wet with seawater as the two friends walked along the lumpy street towards the castle.

'Maybe it's your parents?' suggested Wynn.

Casper nodded. 'She did say something about respecting their wishes, but why? It's not like they're close. Why should she care what they want?'

'And your granny has no idea you've been training with her ex?'

'No.' Casper cringed with shame. The trophies were one thing, but the photos of Ida and Beryl felt more private.

'Well, that could be awkward.'

'She doesn't ask many questions,' he continued. 'I think she knows it'll only end with me demanding some answers of my own.'

'It all sounds very dramatic,' said Wynn. 'Is it worth the hassle? What if something goes wrong, or you have an accident? Your granny will feel terrible, and your parents will probably blame her!'

'Nothing is going to go wrong,' insisted Casper. 'Once I've swum the Channel she'll be proud. She'll see that banning me from swimming was a mistake – no matter what my parents' problem is.'

'Maybe nothing's gone wrong *yet*, but there's still

the curse, remember?'

Casper ignored her, rolling his eyes while she continued to rant about the many misfortunes of Channel-swimming children. Despite the things he'd seen in Corallium, from the swirling vortex to the vision of coral in Ida's closet, he was still having trouble believing that some ancient power might have a problem with him breaking an old swimming record. He'd been training with Beryl for this long and had no issue, after all . . .

They approached a bend in the pockmarked road, and the four rugged spires of Corallium Castle lifted into view.

'It's along here,' said Wynn, pulling Casper on to the grass and down a narrow slope.

'I thought your dad was digging by the castle?'

'He was, but they found something which led them here. He made me promise that we'd come and see today.'

The pair stumbled through the slippery woodland that grew in the shadow of the castle, jumping over boulders and bushes and ducking under the slick leaves of the trees until they left the mossy under-growth for open air.

'Whoa,' they gulped in unison, stunned at the sight which greeted them.

Ahead lay an enormous crater dug from the earth and at its centre, a thick pink ripple of coral cut through the ground like an artery. Despite its stillness, Casper could've imagined it a living, breathing organism – as if it were the swollen limb of some great subterranean octopus. It seemed to radiate with energy.

'Kids!' a cheery voice called from the pit, and Dev appeared in a luminous yellow jacket. A row of tools swung from the belt around his waist, and on his head he wore a knitted tea cosy. He patted the strange pink pipe gently and beamed up at them. 'Isn't it incredible?'

'What *is* it?' asked Wynn, her eyes as wide as Casper's – which felt larger than the deep hole that lay before them.

'Can't you tell?' asked Tan, appearing over the ridge of the crater. He frowned, seeing that his sister had brought a friend.

'It's the castle . . .' said Casper, ignoring Tan's frosty welcome and craning his neck towards the craggy turrets that loomed above them.

'Got it in one,' smiled Dev.

'The castle?' gasped Wynn, scratching her head as she followed Casper's eyeline. 'But how can that be possible?'

'These are the foundations, or the roots, as I've been calling them. The town was literally built on top of this coral reef, with that incredible castle-like formation at its centre. Branches of coral, like this one, run from the core and across the whole area like a nervous system. They are the veins of Corallium, and once upon a time might have powered every living part of this landscape.'

'So the castle *is* alive,' whispered Casper, awestruck.

'Maybe dormant,' Dev continued. 'We're closer to sea down here, but the castle will have dried out over thousands of years.'

Wynn jumped into the crater and jogged to her brother. They examined the tentacle up close, while Casper looked back to the greying spires above them. His heart ached. The castle ruins had inspired him with wonder before, but now he knew the truth, they were even more beautiful in a melancholic kind of way. He pictured how they might have looked a thousand years ago, underwater and blushing pink like the vision of coral he'd seen in Ida's closet.

The closet . . .

The guilt thumped his insides again.

'How do you like my hat?' asked Dev, calling Casper's attention. 'Elsie was furious when she saw me on the high street. I beat her at the bingo again.'

'It's great,' laughed Casper. 'Though I think it's meant for a teapot.'

'Oh, well, that explains the hole.' Dev pulled the knitted cosy over his face, and his nose popped through a seam like a short china spout. 'I'm glad Wynn brought you down this afternoon,' he mumbled behind the wool. 'There's something extra-special that I want us all to uncover together. Come this way.'

Casper climbed down and joined Wynn and Tan, before they followed Dev to the far side of the basin. A yellow digger waited with a young woman sitting at the controls. She wore a pair of khaki shorts and a green T-shirt underneath a luminous jacket to match Dev's. On her head was a yellow hard hat, and her hand rested on the control stick of the machine.

'This is my assistant, Jack,' said Dev.

'Hi, guys,' she smiled from the seat. 'You're just in time.'

'Hi, Jack,' said Casper and Wynn.

'What are we meant to be looking at?' asked Tan, nonplussed. He folded his arms and pulled on a pair of sunglasses.

'That slab of rock,' said Wynn, pointing to the wall of the crater. Casper could just about make out the rectangular shape of a tall brown stone, camouflaged against the earth.

'That's right,' smiled Dev. He brushed the side of the slab with a gloved hand, and Casper realized it was framed by a zigzag mosaic of faded pink and orange shells. The border felt oddly familiar.

'Jack is going to move it for us,' continued Dev.

Jack turned a key and the digger's engine started with a low grumble. 'If your dad is right, there might be something pretty special waiting on the other side.'

'I'm always right.'

'What's on the other side? More coral?' asked Casper.

'I'd wager something even more exciting,' beamed Dev.

'You *did* wager,' said Jack, while Dev pulled open a dusty duffel bag. He tossed the children a pair of protective goggles and a yellow hard hat each, securing one on top of his own head which squished the tea cosy down on to his hair.

'Whenever you're ready, Jack!'

'Keep back,' she shouted, rolling the digger slowly towards the edge of the crater. Using a lever in her left hand Jack twisted the cabin to face the large slab, and with one in her right brought the large yellow shovel at the front of the machine up to meet the ridge of the earth. It raked the dirt with its claw-like teeth before hooking on to the topmost edge of the tall stone. 'Ready in three . . .

'Two . . .

'One . . .'

Jack pushed the lever and the bucket curled behind the slab, which shuddered against the tightly packed earth before slowly breaking away from its bed of soil. It gave in to the force of the digger, spluttering as sand and dirt crumbled around its edges while the stone came loose. The slab fell forward and landed at Dev's feet with a colossal crash.

Casper strained his eyes through the dust and saw

that a large hole had been left in its place. 'A corridor!' he gasped.

Dev scurried forward, while Jack hopped down from the digger. 'I suppose I owe you a drink now, Dev.'

'There are stairs carved from the chalk in the soil,' said Tan, giving in to his curiosity at last. 'Where does it lead?'

'Let's take a look,' smiled Dev. He turned on a lamp at the front of his hard hat and took a step inside, followed closely by his son who still wore sunglasses beneath his clear goggles. Wynn held back, looking down the staircase with apprehension.

'Are we sure this is a good idea?'

Jack ran a hand around the rim of the doorway. 'It looks to be structurally sound. This passageway must have been built by someone highly skilled.'

'Or *something*,' Dev's voiced echoed back along the passage. 'You have to come and take a look at this!'

Jack, Wynn and Casper scrambled through the doorway, their own headlights illuminating the narrow staircase roughly hewn from the chalk. After half a dozen steps, Dev and Tan came back into view.

'What the—'

At the bottom of the staircase, two tunnels curved out to form a circular passageway around a thick central column. But it wasn't merely this which took Casper's breath away. The walls and ceiling were adorned with thousands upon thousands of shells, which delicately decorated the entire hallway in intricate patterns and shapes.

Casper followed Wynn down the left-side passage, while the others turned right.

'This is incredible,' choked Wynn. 'What does it mean?'

'I don't know,' Casper whispered in reply. His eyes scanned the walls for every last detail of the grand mosaic which stretched along the entire tunnel. Spirals of cockle shells swirled down the walls like waves and were topped by limpets as white as sea foam. Mussels were fanned in circular patterns like rays of sunshine, and every gap was filled by clams and whelks of all shapes and sizes.

'How can no one have known about this?' asked Casper.

Wynn shrugged. 'I guess my dad is the first person barmy enough to have dug up the foundations of Corallium Castle.'

They continued to follow the wall until the two tunnels met to form a square atrium about the size of Ida's ground floor. Dev, Jack and Tan had appeared from the other side of the passage and were already staring at the domed ceiling in awe.

Dev swallowed, and his gulp echoed in the silence.

'When we uncovered the coral veins and found that slab with the mosaic border, I suspected it might conceal some kind of passage . . . but *this*!' He gazed around the atrium in disbelief, wiping his brow. 'I never imagined we'd make a discovery such as this.'

Dolphins and whales swam across the walls with scallop fins and oyster-pearl eyes, while even more shells in massive swathes of colour covered every space in between.

Jack continued to study them up close. 'The shells are all local. They'd have been easy to find in such quantities several centuries ago.'

'This is what we've been searching for,' smiled Dev.

'What do you mean?' asked Casper.

'It could be proof,' said Jack. 'A city that once belonged to the sea, pushed up through the waves and brought to land like a beached whale.'

'It's hardly *proof*,' said Tan. His voice betrayed a level of wonder.

'No, but it's a start!' replied Dev. His excitement felt infectious, though Casper was distracted as his eyes found the floor of the room.

Two large intertwining spirals were carved in the ground like the ripples of an enormous whirlpool. He suddenly felt dizzy as a sense of déjà vu overwhelmed him – the memory of Ida's flooded entrance hall engulfed his brain. The carving was exactly the same size and shape as the sinking vortex which he'd thought he'd imagined.

The floor seemed to drop beneath him.

'If Corallium was really a city underwater, what happened to the people who lived there?' asked Wynn, unaware of the change in Casper.

'Maybe they're out in the ocean somewhere,' suggested Jack.

'Or maybe as their home changed, over time, they were forced to change as well,' added Dev. 'It would have taken thousands of years for the seabed to rise above the water and drain this grotto. Who knows how these people might have adapted to survive?'

The conversation began to fade away as Casper knelt, his head spinning.

'What are you doing?' asked Tan, squinting distrustfully. His eyes scanned the floor, widening at the sight of the large carvings which spun from the centre.

'They're making me feel woozy,' said Casper.

'Whoa,' said Wynn, as she too looked to the ground. She backed away and leant on the wall for support. 'It's like the floor is sinking.'

Casper nodded, while Tan stared at the carving in a trance.

'Casper!' yelled Dev, suddenly serious. 'You're very pale. What's wrong?'

'It's the floor,' said Wynn.

Dev glanced at the spirals but was unaffected. 'We need to get you back to the surface for some fresh air.' He helped Casper up and began to lead him back towards the circular hallway.

'I think there's a quicker way,' said Jack, looking up and down the room. 'You see those pink and orange shells?'

Casper followed Jack's finger and saw the same zigzag pattern from the stone slab also bordered a tall, rectangular mosaic at the centre of the wall.

'A door?' asked Dev, impressed.

'This pattern seems to indicate an entry point. Judging by the length of the tunnels, I'd say we must be approaching the cliff face. If I just—'

Jack examined the wall and found a small hollow with her hand, which she used to gently pull the door. After a moment, the chalk wall groaned and began to move slowly inwards. The dim glow of distant daylight found its way through the crack.

'Jack, you genius!' smiled Dev. He joined her at the doorway and helped to tug it open, before the pair scrambled through. Wynn and Tan went next, and when Casper followed he found himself crawling through layers of wild shrubbery until he finally flopped on to sand.

'We're in the heather,' said Wynn with a laugh. 'The grotto brought us all the way to the sea!'

The sound of waves filled Casper's ears, and the breeze blew flecks of gold down from the dunes which stood between him and the water. Dev and Jack were already heading back inside the grotto to continue exploring, while Casper's feet tingled with a realization.

'Ida's front door,' he said with a gasp, finally

understanding why the pink and orange border of the entryways seemed so familiar.

He turned to look up the cliffs and was stunned to see the towering shape of Ida's strange home looming high above the heather – directly over the grotto. Pink coral crept up the sides of the building like curious hands, and over the roof the billowing white sails of a colossal ship were once again slicing through the sky.

CHAPTER EIGHTEEN

Brakes and Adders

Countless thoughts still crashed through Casper's head a few days after their discovery of the grotto. Its stone doorways were decorated just like Ida's front door, and the atrium, with its swirling spirals, sat directly beneath her house!

Was this the reason he kept having strange visions of the building, as if seeing it from the sea floor? The images of flying sails and creeping coral were infrequent, but Casper was surer than ever that they weren't a trick of his mind.

Dev had banned them from returning to the grotto while he carried on his excavation, and Casper was furious with himself for letting the stone spirals make him dizzy. There was *so* much more they could have explored together, and he had so many un-answered questions.

'You've a lot on your mind today,' said Beryl, tread-ing water at the end of another training session.

'It's nothing,' Casper fibbed. While the grotto had been a distraction all day, his swimming was also a reminder of the golden trophies and trinkets stashed in Ida's cupboard like a dirty secret.

'I know when something's up,' pressed Beryl. 'The sea may be a bit choppy, but that's no excuse for your breathing. It's like you've forgotten you even need oxygen, the way you're charging forward without so much as a glug of air for twenty-odd strokes.'

Casper blushed, looking back along the beach towards *Les Moules-Frites* where he saw Wynn lying on her surfboard in the water. She paddled forward with both arms, finally jumping to her feet as the board caught a wave which carried her into the shore.

The rest of the seafront was empty, except for a bald man leaving the water near the beach huts. His baggy swimming shorts hung from his bony frame like clothes on a washing line. The old man picked up a cup from the sand and sucked on the straw with huge effort.

'You're distracted,' continued Beryl, now certain that Casper's mind was elsewhere. 'Swimming is the best way to clear your thoughts and let go of all the heavy stuff. If a six-hour session hasn't helped, then maybe talking will.'

Casper chewed his lip, considering, while an irritating hum began to vibrate through his head . . . Beryl would think he was mad if he told her about the phantom whirlpool or sails, but maybe she could help him understand the treasure trove in Ida's hallway cupboard.

And the photos.

'CASPER! GET OUT OF THE WAY!' shouted Beryl.

He turned in the water, the humming noise now louder than even the waves on which he saw the unmanned jet ski charging straight towards him. It crashed through the sea, firing white foam in every direction, unrelenting in its course, which was a straight line targeting Casper's face.

'DUCK!'

He felt Beryl's hands on his shoulders as they pulled him beneath the water. Casper looked up to the surface in the same moment that the white belly of the speeding jet ski soared over – only centimetres above his head. A moment later Beryl released her grip, allowing him to break through the waves with a gasp.

'Deep breaths, lad,' said Beryl. 'Slow an' steady. That's it.'

Casper's nostrils felt like fire – there'd been no time to breathe before he'd found himself under-water. He saw the jet ski shoot across the shallows and collide with the beach, where it skidded over the sand like a skimming stone. Finally it came to a halt, crash-ing into a large dune with a bang.

Beryl led Casper on to the beach and once they reached the jet ski, which buzzed angrily like a trapped wasp, she leant over and pressed a red button poking from the sand. The engine fell silent.

'What on earth—' she said, pulling the machine from its perch. 'The accelerator seems to have been damaged.' Beryl flicked a plastic trigger on the handlebar back and forth. It flopped about lifelessly.

'Casper, are you OK?' asked Wynn, arriving at his side with her surfboard.

'Just a little shaken.'

'I'll pop the kettle on,' said Beryl. 'I think we've earnt a rest!' She dragged the jet ski over to the beach huts and Casper watched in silent awe – still astounded by her strength.

'That was scary,' said Wynn. 'I saw the whole thing. It came out of nowhere and hurtled straight for you!'

'I know,' replied Casper. 'It just appeared; I don't know what happened. Who was steering it anyway?'

'I didn't see anyone,' said Wynn, her brow wrinkled with concern. 'It would've been nasty if Beryl hadn't warned you. You don't think it could have been . . .' She trailed off.

'What?'

'Never mind,' she said cagily. 'I'm going to change out of this wetsuit. I'll see you in a minute.'

She ran down the beach, and Casper collapsed into one of the stripy deck chairs outside Beryl's beach hut. He heard the click of the gas hob being turned off, followed by the clattering of china. A moment later

Beryl appeared with a tray holding a bright pink teapot, several mugs and the obligatory packet of chocolate biscuits.

'We should let your gran know what's happened,' she said, lowering herself into a deck chair.

'No!' yelled Casper. 'I'm fine, really. There's no reason to get her down here.' He looked to the ground, hiding his guilty face from Beryl's probing eyes.

'She's not still giving you a hard time about the swimmin'?'

'Not exactly,' countered Casper. He decided not to mention the fact that Ida was still in the dark about his Channel training, never mind that he'd been banned from the water entirely!

'Then what's going on?' asked Beryl. 'I feel like you were just about to tell me something before that jet ski came careering down the seafront.'

Casper sighed. If there was anyone who understood his need to be by the water it was Beryl, and she'd known his grandmother for so much longer than he had...

He felt himself give way to the need for answers.

'I was here in Corallium before, as a baby,' he

started. 'Living or visiting, I'm not sure. Granny says there are things I can't know, or else my parents will never let me come back again.'

Beryl frowned curiously and began to pour from the teapot. After filling two mugs and adding a dash of milk to both, she passed one to Casper who sat there fizzing with frustration.

'There's something else,' he said. 'The two of you don't even talk . . . but before I arrived, she had all these pictures of you hanging around the house. Photos of your adventures across the country, in fancy frames. Now the walls are bare and marked with dark, shadowy patches. It's like she's ashamed.'

Beryl took a long, loud glug of her tea.

'Ida wants—' Casper stopped himself, '*wanted* me to give up my dream of breaking Bernie's record . . . But she has an entire cupboard filled with ribbons, trophies and gold medals – all for swimming!' He snorted at the irony, finally looking up to meet Beryl's eyes.

He wanted to trust her. He wanted to tell her all about the coral room in Ida's home, the shell grotto beneath it and his brilliant webbed toes . . .

'And—'

The words caught in his throat, unable to find their way on to his tongue to form a sentence.

Beryl broke the silence with another long sip of her tea. 'If those pictures have been taken down and her trophies hidden away, it's because Ida doesn't want you seeing them,' she said reprovingly. 'You should know better than to go rifling through people's things.'

'I know,' said Casper, hanging his head. 'But I would have loved having you as my step-granny. I can't think of anything cooler!'

He really couldn't. Casper had idolized Beryl for such a long time. The idea she had once been a member of the family, before he'd even known her, blew his mind.

'But I'm not,' said Beryl. 'I haven't been your step-gran since the day your grandmother swore off swimmin' and never came back down that woodland path again. I understand why you're feeling so much, Casper – but this . . . this really isn't my story to tell.'

'But—'

'No.' Beryl held her hands up like a full stop. 'You've got to trust your granny. I can't speak for her, but I can promise that she loves you dearly and has your best interests at heart.'

They sat in silence, finishing their tea. Wynn was finally walking towards them down the beach, wearing a dry T-shirt and shorts. She waved.

'That reminds me, actually,' started Beryl, standing up. She rummaged in a cupboard and returned to her deck chair with a Channel Swimming Syndicate mug. 'This is Ida's one. Can you pop it back inside where you found it?'

Waving to Wynn, Casper took the mug next door to Ida's beach hut, which he'd unlocked earlier, and stood on his sandy tiptoes to reach the cupboard door.

When the door swung open, he yelped.

The grass snake had returned.

'What's wrong?' called Wynn. She had arrived outside and already made herself comfortable in Casper's empty deck chair.

'Nothing,' he laughed, his heart racing from the slight shock of another slithering surprise. 'That grass snake has managed to get back inside Ida's cupboard, that's all.'

'How weird.' He heard Wynn's voice, confused and muffled through the curtain. 'I thought I'd patched up the hole pretty well – it shouldn't have been able to.'

Casper shook his head, seeing that the rocks Wynn had left at the back of the cupboard to cover the hole were still in place. But the snake had made its way in somehow . . . He shrugged. It was harmless, after all. Why not leave it to go about its business?

He stretched his arm up to the cupboard, watching while the reptile coiled its body around the old copper kettle. The striking black zigzag on the snake's patterned back reflected in the warped metal like a fun-house mirror . . . But that wasn't right. The grass snake he'd seen before had been a similar greenish brown, but patterned with short, bar-like markings.

And the grass snake hadn't hissed.

It hadn't turned to face him with bulging red eyes, its black, forked tongue poking from thin lips like an angry whip.

The grass snake hadn't had two white fangs—

'Casper, no!' cried Wynn. She appeared in the doorway and batted his arm aside. The mug flew from Casper's hand and smashed against the wall of the beach hut, breaking into a dozen pieces in the very same moment that the snake sprang forward.

Its jaw missed Casper's outstretched fingers by a hair's breadth.

Wynn flew to the cupboard doors and slammed them shut on the now livid, and still hissing, snake. 'Are you OK?' she asked, grabbing Casper's hand to examine it for punctures.

'I'm fine, I'm fine, but what did I do wrong? I thought you said it was harmless.'

'Grass snakes are,' Wynn breathed. 'But that was an adder! They keep to themselves but this one was cornered. It would have felt pretty threatened when you got in its face.'

'An adder? They're venomous!' panicked Casper, realizing how close he'd come to disaster. 'It almost bit me! How did it get inside?'

'Through the hole, I guess. I must have done a real botch-job fixing it.'

'But you didn't,' continued Casper, sweating. 'Before the adder struck I saw the hole was still covered up.'

'That makes no sense,' said Wynn.

Casper sloped on to the seafront, the adrenaline draining as he walked towards the water. 'If that snake had bitten me it could have ended my training!'

'You're right,' said Wynn, her eyes filled with clarity. 'It's starting.'

'What?'

'The adder. That jet ski . . . Accidents that have no rhyme or reason; hazards appearing out of thin air, don't you see? This is only the beginning.'

'Of what?' demanded Casper.

'It's happening, and it's going to make sure your Channel swim is stopped in its tracks. Just like with my brother. Just like Julia Bellwether, Jeremy Jones and all the rest.'

Casper shuddered in spite of himself. 'I've told you; I don't believe in cur—'

He stopped short, stunned into silence.

Two large intertwining spirals had been drawn in the wet sand like graffiti. Casper couldn't help but gulp as he stepped backwards, once again feeling the familiar sensation of falling through an enormous, spinning whirlpool – this one a sinking swirl of yellow.

He held his knees, and Wynn exhaled sharply.

'Casper, it's just like the carving in the shell grotto,' she said, lowering her voice as she looked about suspiciously. 'How is this here?'

'Someone is messing with us,' said Casper. He righted himself and focused his eyes on the horizon line, his sharp spell of dizziness fading.

'But we're the only people who know about the grotto. My dad and Jack are there again today, and Tan doesn't come down here any more. Not since his swim—'

'But I saw him once,' said Casper. 'On my first day of training with Beryl. I forgot to tell you because it was just before I found the grass snake and uncovered the patterned carpet.' His eyes widened. 'You don't think that Tan . . .'

Wynn frowned. 'He'll hate me for telling you, but I think he's jealous of your plan to break the record.'

'So he has a motive. Maybe he's trying to scare me off?'

Wynn shook her head firmly. 'I don't think he'd want to frighten us. He might be traumatized by mackerel, but he's not a bad person.'

'A double spiral won't have appeared in the sand by magic,' said Casper.

'Why not?' insisted Wynn. 'It's not a coincidence that every child who ever tries to swim the Channel fails miserably . . . Now this appears? What if the curse and the shell grotto are connected?'

Casper felt another involuntary tremor run down his spine, because he knew that Wynn was on to something – even though she didn't quite know the truth of why.

The grotto, his family, the ocean and his feet . . .

They were all connected.

He just wasn't sure how.

CHAPTER NINETEEN

The Red Sea

Just as Wynn had promised, Casper's near misses with the runaway jet ski and a venomous adder had only been the start.

A few days later, while Wynn and Beryl pottered about inside her beach hut, Casper quietly allowed his enormous feet to fly free. Skimming his webbed toes through the sand as he bounded across the dunes to the water, suddenly, before he could stop himself, he was falling through the air in slow motion. His long feet had clipped a rock half-buried in the sand, causing him to tumble head first to the ground with a great clatter . . .

A lucky escape, it turned out.

'I could've broken my leg!' Casper ranted, pointing at the enormous hole dug in the sand right next to where he'd landed, and covered suspiciously by a shortbread-coloured towel. He batted Beryl away when she attempted to examine his sandy feet for injury. 'I said *could've*, I'm fine – honest!'

Later that same week, after lathering himself in thick suntan lotion, Casper had spent his rest day with Wynn, reading on the beach . . . But it wasn't until Corallium's entire population of seagulls was clawing at Casper's back that he'd realized the tube's contents had been switched with goose fat from Beryl's private stash.

'You don't honestly believe that all these accidents are the work of some special hex reserved for under-twelves?' he asked Wynn a few moments later, scrubbing the goo from his skin in the sea. 'Would a water god or ocean nymph really care this much about Channel-swimming children? We only just uncovered the grotto. How could it be linked when your "curse" has been maiming swimmers for sixty-odd years?'

Wynn thought about this for a moment. 'It's true that the others didn't have *quite* as much bad luck as you . . . And I don't just mean that riptide on Tuesday.'

'It would've washed me right out to sea if you hadn't got me on your board and paddled us out of the current,' sighed Casper.

'When a riptide forms Beryl always marks it with a flag, but that day it just vanishes?' Wynn questioned. 'Then there's that random smack of jellyfish too.'

Casper winced, remembering the pain of being caught in the middle of the shoal. He was filled with gratitude for Beryl. She had been there to drag him from the water *again*, and thankfully also helped dispel the myth of Wynn's miracle cure for jellyfish stings . . .

'They're never like that here,' she continued. 'Every other swimmer has had one weird accident while crossing the Channel. You've had loads, and you're only training! I'm just saying, maybe you should think about calling this off—'

Casper gasped.

'I *know* you can do it,' said Wynn, her hands up. 'But is it really worth the risk?'

He stared at her glumly, no longer enjoying the lapping of the cool waves on his cleaned back. Whether Casper believed in curses or not, one thing remained certain. He had been born for swimming, and a series of peculiar accidents would not be enough to end his dream of crossing the Channel.

'I'm not giving up,' he insisted. 'I've worked too hard to stop now.'

The following day, ignoring the niggling voice in his ear, Casper left Ida's rundown beach hut in his home-made swimming trunks – a long thread swinging down by his knees.

Beryl glanced at them disapprovingly. 'Those old leggings are on their last breath,' she said. 'I suppose it's a good thing that these have arrived.' She rummaged inside her carpet bag and pulled out a small brown package, which she threw to Casper.

Heart pounding, he tore the paper open to find a brand-new pair of shiny swimming trunks. They were cobalt blue, with small yellow tridents stitched on each hip which shot thin bolts of lightning up the seam. It was the best gift ever.

A real pair of trunks.

'Thank you so much, Beryl,' he beamed.

'Well, get them on and let's get you in that water!'

Once he'd changed, Casper ran to the edge of the sand and stepped in. This was his favourite moment, when the cold water would wash across his webbed feet and take the heavy sand he used for a shield with it. He fanned his toes happily, without a soul around to see the thick band of skin that connected each one like a pink concertina beneath the waves.

After savouring the feeling for a moment, Casper dove into the waves.

He swam a few strokes, treading water when the seabed sank away beneath him into a green and misty haze. He floated on the surface, waiting for Beryl to give him the go-ahead.

Something felt odd.

Dozens of tiny fish were swimming about his waist . . . more than he'd ever seen in the English Channel, let alone this close without them rushing away in a shimmer of silver. They swam through his legs and all around, their thrashing bodies twisting through the water like twinkling bullets.

'What the—'

Casper looked back to shore and saw Wynn walk across the sand with Tan and their father, Dev. They arrived at the beach huts, a surfboard under Wynn's arm as they began to talk with Beryl and pointed out to sea in his direction. Dev gesticulated nervously, sometimes scratching his head.

What's going on? thought Casper. *Why is Tan here?*

He spun in the water, following their stares, and saw it. An abandoned rowing boat, drifting on the water not far from where he floated. He swam towards it, his curiosity piqued, and once he drew closer Casper realized the boat was leaking...

Odd, for something made to keep the water out to have its own cargo dribble from a hole in the hull like a freshly made wound. It smelt funny too. Like an old fishmonger rotting in the midday sun, and once Casper finally reached the boat he was horrified to see that the liquid inside was a deep red.

Blood.

Casper gagged as he saw the boat was filled with old fish heads and other foul things that were slowly trickling into the sea. It was sending the small fish into a feeding frenzy and suddenly, a much larger haddock slammed into Casper's front. He was winded by the impact, wheezing for air while the silver fish continued to swirl about him. Once he caught his breath Casper's stomach proceeded to drop, dizzy as if he'd found himself standing above the grotto's stone spiral.

This was wrong. So wrong.

He had to move away from the boat, quickly.

Then, a chorus of voices called from the shore. They grew and grew, becoming frantic shouts and screams that were louder and more urgent with every note.

'CASPER!'

'GET OUT!'

He turned again to spot Beryl, Wynn and Dev, now at the water's edge, their feet in the shallows and their arms waving furiously. Tan stood further back towards the beach huts, his face as pale as the phantom sails over Ida's home.

Wynn brandished her surfboard in the air.

'CASPER!'

'SHARK!'

Shark? But that was ridiculous. He wasn't

swimming off the coast of Cape Town or Perth. This was *Corallium*.

Though he did feel strange.

The fish rushing about his waist had suddenly disappeared. The liquid continued to flow from the sinking boat nearby, turning the seawater a pale red. Casper's nose was filled with the sharp scent of metal as he turned and finally saw . . . the unmistakeable, exceptionally large fin of a grey fish slicing through the waves towards him.

A shark.

'SWIM, CASPER!' Beryl and Dev cried from the beach. Their hands, no longer pointing, were clasped instead to their foreheads in panic.

Casper threw his face in the water and swam, faster and more furiously than he'd ever swum in his life. He could feel the presence of his unseen enemy racing behind. His webbed toes flapped, pounding the water like two large propellor blades while fighting the urge to withdraw and nestle in close to the rest of Casper's body.

He wasn't going to make it. He was still too slow, and the beach too far away.

Then suddenly, the shark was in front of him.

Casper stopped and the panic rose in his chest. The shark began to circle, tasting the water and trying to decide what kind of fish Casper might be and whether or not he would make a good meal. The circle drew closer and closer, before the shark's long nose finally brushed Casper's body. He was frozen, unable to move for fear of what a sudden kick or dive might force the shark to do. And then . . .

BONK!

A surfboard appeared from nowhere and rammed the shark on the nose, knocking it sideways with a painful thump. It was Wynn. She was beside Casper in the water, lying on her board, which she pulled him on to, before using her arms to quickly paddle through the water and towards the beach.

Casper turned back and saw the shark limping sadly back to the sinking boat, looking about as confused as Casper felt himself, and when the surfboard reached the shallows Beryl heaved him on to the sand. Dev and Tan ran over.

'Are you OK?' asked Beryl, kneeling beside him. She patted him down, looking for any sign of a bite mark.

'I'm fine,' he panted, crashing as the adrenaline left his body.

'Thanks to Wynn,' cheered Dev. He slapped her on the back approvingly. 'That shark didn't know what hit it! Nobody messes with my daughter and a surfboard.'

Wynn smiled, her cheeks red despite the cold water.

'The poor thing was just confused,' said Beryl. 'Lord knows how it ended up all the way down here.'

'I know, a shark! Wow,' whistled Dev. 'I've never heard of anything quite like it.'

'Me neither,' said Beryl, pursing her lips in deep thought.

Casper was shocked. If even she had never heard of such a thing, what were the chances that a shark would find its way here now? While *he* was in the water? He exchanged a glance with Wynn, who mouthed the word, 'Curse.'

A chill ran down his spine.

'That was really scary,' whispered Tan. The colour was still drained from his face.

'What was in that boat?' asked Beryl.

'The boat . . .' Casper repeated, looking down at his legs. They were tinged with red. 'It was full of old fish. Guts, heads and other horrible stuff. It was leaking out of a hole in the boat – I guess that's what attracted the shark.'

'Gross!' said Wynn.

'How did a boat filled with old fish get out on the water?' asked Dev, the question a mixture of curiosity and concern.

'And more importantly, why?' finished Beryl.

To put my life in danger, Casper answered in his head. Thoughts were spilling over one another like the bulkheads of a buckling ship. Something was definitely trying to stop him swimming the English Channel, even if that meant his life was on the line.

Something or *someone*.

CHAPTER TWENTY

The Curse Uncovered

The next morning, Casper and Wynn stopped short at the sight of the newspaper's front page:

SHARK MISSING FROM AQUARIUM IN BIZARRE BURGLARY

The sleepy town was shaken by the sighting of a shark in its shallow waters, the first such incident in more than seventy years – according to Bertha Vale, anyway. At an emergency town meeting, she claimed her childhood sweetheart Henry had been swallowed whole by a great white shark.

'All that was left was his polka dot swimming trunks!'

Her claim was quickly debunked, when someone pointed out to Bertha that her husband, Henry, was sitting right beside her.

Wynn and Casper pored over the newspaper, sitting on the grass in the shadow of Corallium Castle which towered above their heads like the crown of an ocean king.

'Why would someone steal a *shark*, just to throw it back in the sea?' asked Wynn, putting the paper down. 'It has to be the curse. How else do you explain it?'

Casper looked at the castle's craggy turrets and wondered whether the shark had felt the same desperate urge to be near Corallium that he did. He shook his head and picked up the paper. 'It says here the police have a lead – a bald man seen loitering about the aquarium. If it's really the same shark from the beach then the theft was the work of a human. Maybe an animal activist wanted to release it back into the wild?'

'Off the coast of Corallium? Not the best place for a reef shark to set up home.'

'But fish *do* belong in the sea,' asserted Casper, setting down the paper. 'Can you imagine what it's like to be torn from the ocean and lobbed into a tank for people to gawp at all day long?' He thought back to his parents' desperate pleas for him to keep his webbed feet undercover, their greatest fear being that Casper would end up in a glass tank of his own. 'Being kept from the sea was bad enough for *me* – and I walk on two legs.'

'It's nice to think the thief set the shark free,' said Wynn. 'But how can you explain the blood-filled boat? We're lucky Tan saw it and came to find my dad.'

'Tan?' asked Casper.

'That's why we were there. Tan saw the leaking boat from the cliffs and had a bad feeling.'

Casper squinted, unconvinced. The rowing boat had been far too small to give Tan the heebie-jeebies from the top of the woodland path. How far might his jealousy have driven him? Casper had seen him lurking on the beach once before. Could claiming he'd had a hand in the rescue be a big distraction?

Wynn folded the paper, suddenly brightening. 'I know where we might find some answers. Come with me.'

Casper followed her along the winding shell-paved streets. Eventually they came to a stop outside an old stone building, which looked like a messy pile of pebbles. Casper supposed that it would've made the perfect home for all sorts of creatures when the town had been on the bottom of the sea. He read the sign above the door:

'Corallium Library?'

'They've loads of old newspapers,' answered Wynn. 'We can have a rummage and see whether anything connects all the failed attempts to break Bernie's Channel record.'

Casper was surprised. 'I thought you were certain it was all down to some curse?'

'Well . . . you've made me wonder,' said Wynn, noticing his expression. 'But don't look too smug! It's still possible.'

Inside, a small woman sat behind the reception desk, reading. An enormous pair of glasses magnified her eyes to the size of saucepans, and her blueish hair was held in place with a yellow pencil. She ushered them over with a gentle wave.

'Shh!' she said, in a rather loud, exaggerated stage whisper.

'We didn't say anything,' replied Casper matter-of-factly.

'And there's no one else here,' added Wynn, indicating the empty room with a flail of her arm. Several tables were scattered with dusty books, but each one was vacant.

'Sorry, force of habit,' the librarian said. She marked her place in her novel with a bookmark and set it on the counter. The cover depicted a man with long blonde hair embracing a woman on a beach bathed in the orange glow of sunset. 'My name is Vera. What can I do for you, dears? Romance, is it? That's shelves one through seventy-two.'

'Um, no,' said Wynn quickly. 'We wanted to look through some old newspapers.'

'Oh, yes?' said Vera, raising her eyebrows with interest. 'Are you researching a summer project on the history of Corallium?'

'Something like that,' smiled Casper, catching Wynn's eye.

'You'll find everything downstairs – this whole

floor is fiction. Well, it's all romance, come to think of it.'

Following the librarian's directions, Casper and Wynn went down into a draughty cellar. Water dripped from the ceiling and landed in a rusty bucket on the floor, which wafted the smell of the sea towards them. Most of the room was taken up with several rows of thick metal shelving, which were tightly packed together.

'How are we meant to get down the aisles?' asked Casper.

'By using the rails,' answered Wynn. She pointed to the base of the shelving units and Casper saw they were fixed to train-like tracks. Wynn walked to the far shelf and turned a large wheel attached to its side. The shelf began to roll along the track, granting access to the much-widened aisle.

'Let's get to work,' she said, running a finger down a paper list which she pulled from her pocket. 'Samuel Seabury's attempt to swim the Channel was ten years ago. The other cases we've identified are all within the previous fifty – and one was just *two weeks* after Bernie's record-breaking swim.'

'Who was that?' asked Casper.

'Irene Ingleby,' said Wynn. 'Her support boat sank mid-swim after some kind of accident. The whole team was rescued from the sea.'

'And it was only two weeks after Bernie's swim? I bet he *hated* the thought of someone stealing his thunder so quickly.'

Before long, they were lying on the floor of the basement surrounded by piles of ageing newspapers. They riffled through the pages, looking for any information they could find on the ill-fated Channel swims of every child they knew about.

'Here,' said Wynn suddenly. She pointed at the yellowing copy of the *Corallium Times* in front of her. Casper saw the headline in large black letters:

A HAIR'S BREADTH FROM A RECORD-BREAKING SWIM

'Is that the boy with the mullet?' he asked.

'Yes,' said Wynn, reading the article. 'Jeremy's hair was sucked inside his pilot boat's propellor when it veered off course. Apparently, a replacement skipper was brought in after the original was taken ill...'

Wynn finished reading and tossed the paper to Casper. Inside was a photograph of Jeremy Jones in tears, holding the chewed-up remains of his mullet for the camera. The boat's skipper stood behind him, equally bald, as reporters crowded around him with microphones.

Casper turned back to another paper splayed on the floor. 'How about this one, from twenty years ago. It's about a girl named Desirée Abebe.' He ran a finger down the page to the relevant piece:

PASTRY INSULT CAUSES INTERNATIONAL INCIDENT

'French officials received an anonymous call, telling them that Desirée had once said, "Croissants aren't all that great, actually." They blockaded the Channel.'

'Wow,' said Wynn with a laugh. 'Overreaction much?'

'She wasn't allowed to make the crossing, but she did become the face of Bakewell tarts. Hold on, look at this one . . .' Casper picked up a particularly crispy copy of the *Corallium Times*.

DISASTER IN THE SHIPPING LANES AS INGLEBY'S SWIMMING GLORY SINKS

'Irene Ingleby!' cried Wynn. 'She was the very first

victim of our curse.'

Casper read from the page.

'*Disaster struck yesterday morning when Irene Ingleby was rescued from the Channel, alongside her coach and supporters, following an explosion of goose fat ignited by a discharged flare. The eruption of fat, which had been used by the young swimmer to stave off the cold upon entering the water, ripped through her pilot boat, forcing all passengers to evacuate into the sea.*'

'Oh no,' said Wynn. 'That sounds terrifying! What happened to Irene?'

'*In an ironic twist of fate, Ingleby was rescued from drowning by—*' Casper gasped. He looked to Wynn with wide eyes before continuing. '*Ingleby was rescued from drowning by Bernie "Baby Face" Baxter! The world record holder, only two weeks out from his own Channel swim aged eleven years, eleven months and twenty-nine days, was named a hero for the daring rescue.*'

'Bernie saved her? But how did the flare go off?'

'It doesn't say.' Casper paused. 'That's the end of the article.'

'Hold on,' said Wynn, rummaging on the floor. 'I have the *Merlington Echo* from the same week here, somewhere.' She picked up another paper and flipped through it, landing on a picture of Irene. She scanned the page quickly. '*The flare gun was discharged by accident*. That's all it says.'

'None of this feels like coincidence, or a *curse*,' insisted Casper. 'Somebody was out to get these kids.'

'But what about Jeremy?' asked Wynn. 'That was an accident, the support boat veered off course.'

'Unless . . .' Casper laid out the newspapers side by side, and looked closely at the picture of Jeremy. 'There's his skipper in the background, bald as anything.' He turned to another edition, this one reporting on Julia Bellwether and the woman she had saved after falling overboard. He quickly read the story in his head.

'Here!' He pointed to a picture of Julia. She was helping a woman decked in sparkling jewellery clamber on board a rescue boat, and in the background, an enormous cruise liner loomed above the scene. 'Look at the people leaning over the railings. There's a bald guy in a lumpy brown cardigan . . .'

He began to read: '*While witnesses have been unable to corroborate the story, Lady Barrington-Smythe claimed to have felt a sharp push from behind* before falling head first over the safety railings and into the sea.'

'What?' gasped Wynn.

'She was pushed!' Casper cried, his heart racing. 'I'd bet anything that it's the same bald man in both pictures. He's been behind every accident.'

'But why?' asked Wynn. 'And who is he? This town is home to a million old men and none of them have been inside the shell grotto. How would they know to scare you off by drawing a spiral in the sand?'

She picked up another paper and flicked through. 'This one should have a story on Samuel Seabury and his Vaseline, let's see if—' She stopped short.

'What is it?' asked Casper, concerned.

'It's . . . Ida.'

'What? What about Ida?'

Wynn swallowed hard; her voice caught in her throat. Casper's mind whirred a million miles an hour, and finally, she began to read from the page in her hands:

'*It was double duty for the Channel Swimming Syndicate last Wednesday. Though officials were unable to verify Samuel Seabury's unsuccessful attempt at the crossing, their trip to Corallium did not go to waste.*

'*The same afternoon local resident and decorated swimmer Ida Delmare, AKA the Delmare Dolphin, completed her own swim across the English Channel but was quietly stripped of the achievement soon after—*'

'No!' cried Casper.

'*While the exact circumstances surrounding this development remain unclear, officials have confirmed to this newspaper that Delmare was found to have been in breach of Syndicate rules and will now be banned from all certified Channel-swimming achievements for life . . .*'

Casper began to sweat. He furrowed his brow, the locked hallway cupboard filled with trinkets and trophies flashing before his eyes. Had he seen a Channel medal glimmer among the gold?

Wynn looked up from the paper. 'Casper, your Granny Ida swam the Channel.'

'And cheated.'

CHAPTER TWENTY-ONE

A Perfect Fit

Casper was furious with Ida. She'd asked him to stay on dry land, knowing full well how much he wanted to swim the Channel, and yet – she'd swum the Channel herself! He was desperate to know why she'd broken the rules, and *how* . . . But he was also scared to hear the answer. Whatever the reason Ida had been disqualified, it was likely why she'd turned her back on the water.

And Beryl.

Later, Casper had another restless night – rushing straight to bed after dinner to avoid Ida's probing stare. For hours he listened to the sound of the waves, drifting in and out of stunted dreams where shining medals cracked in two and bled liquid gold from the wound.

Ida was his grandmother, and now more than ever he was certain that she must feel the same deep longing for the ocean as he did.

And this house?

Even now it seemed like Casper could feel the shell grotto calling up through the floorboards with a pulse that rocked his bed frame and rippled down his webbed feet. The swirling pool of water, the sails flying high above the roof, and the pink coral which he'd seen crawling up the walls of Ida's home.

If his thirst for the water was somehow linked to this house, and Corallium's history, the grotto might hold answers.

There was only one thing for it.

He had to go back.

The first rays of sunlight were slowly casting shadows on the ceiling of the room, which crawled across the paint like trickling water, as Casper rolled from the mattress with a determined puff. He dressed quickly and ran down the stairs, past Ida's open bedroom door without a pause or worry for the noise he made along the way. He grabbed a torch from the kitchen, laced up his heavy shoes and fled the house into the dawn.

Casper made his way through the tall trees and bushes of the woodland walk, which stifled the light in the sun-kissed sky. He knew that Ida, and Dev, would be furious if they knew what he was up to.

But *something* was going on.

The thought pushed him forward as he crawled through the undergrowth towards the cave entrance, camouflaged against the cliff face beneath the towering home of his grandmother. He scoured the rock in the half-light, his nose almost pressed against the wall before he found it – a faded zigzag border of shells in the shape of a door frame.

He placed his shoulder against the rock inside, pushed using his full body weight and after a nervous moment the doorway moved inward with a crunch. The smell of seashells found his nose with a thrill, and he scurried through the gap.

Casper was back inside the atrium.

His torchlight found the stone carvings which spiralled from the centre of the floor before he looked to the ceiling, imagining Ida asleep in her bed a hundred metres or more above him. He knew there must be something down here that tied them both to Corallium.

He just had to find it.

Jack and Dev had taped off sections of the room, the evidence of their work scattered all around in the form of buckets, trowels and brushes set in neat piles. Casper shone his torch along the wall, following the tentacle of an octopus made of periwinkles until the light landed on another doorway slightly ajar and covered by a thin sheet of plastic. A new section of the grotto to explore.

He walked over, pulled back the sheet and slipped through the gap.

Casper gasped.

It was the most elaborately decorated section of the grotto he'd seen. Colossal mosaics of merfolk covered every surface – some with their tails outlined in sharp limpets and with long beards of white razor clams that cascaded down the wall. A narrow shaft rose to the surface, allowing a dim beam of light to break through the shrubbery of the woodland and bathe the room in a ghostly glow.

Casper looked closer at one mosaic and saw that the merfolk's tails ended not with fins, but with large flipper-like feet of pink auger shells – fused at the ankle. His own feet tingled with uncertainty.

What does this mean?

He knelt down, suddenly nauseous, and placed his hands on the floor where they found a ridge protruding from the ground.

Another spiral?

No. It was a mould fossil, similar to the shell-like hollows which littered the pavements of Corallium. But this felt *much* larger. He turned his torch towards it, and another gasp escaped his throat. It wasn't a shell, but a petrified footprint with five long toes, each one joined by thick webbing. Without thinking, Casper tore off his chunky left shoe and placed his own foot into the imprint.

It was a perfect fit.

'It can't be,' he choked, the words barely finding their way into the silent room.

He'd always felt a pull to the water, and Corallium

had felt like home from the moment he'd stepped off the coach . . . but was it possible?

Were the people who had made this grotto like him?

He looked back to the large mosaics, with their sharp whelk frowns and grey limpet eyes which seemed to stare down at him. Their fused feet, and this webbed footprint which still hugged his bare skin, seemed to be proof.

Casper was more connected to this strange place than he could have imagined.

His heart pounded as he crawled back through the bracken to the beach. If the grotto was evidence of an ancient society, then Casper's call to the water made sense for the first time in his life. But if *his* story was this entwined with Corallium's, then so was his family's . . .

And if that were true, his family had been lying about more than his birthplace.

Hoping to suppress the flood of thoughts crashing through his head, Casper climbed the nearest sand dune and looked out to the sea.

He would never tire of the sight.

The deep purple sky, which echoed on the surface like a long-lost twin. The thunderous waves which broke into white horses, frothing crests tumbling forward with the sound of a hundred hooves. The seafront in shadow, and the ocean rising up to caress the sand as it washed the ankles of a person in silhouette . . .

They were back!

Casper inhaled sharply. He'd been so concerned with the 'curse' and the grotto that he'd forgotten all about this person's peculiar morning ritual. But now was his chance to find out who they were.

He slid down the sand dune, keeping low as his questions urged him across the beach and towards the silhouette when suddenly—

Casper's heart stopped as the figure turned to face him.

'Ida!'

CHAPTER TWENTY-TWO

The Family Trait

His grandmother was standing in the water – her nightdress almost brushing the roiling surface. 'Casper, I can explain...' She paused, coming to her senses. 'Hold on. Do you have any idea what time it is? What are you doing here?'

She walked towards him, hesitating only when she reached the edge of the water.

'What are *you* doing here?' asked Casper. 'You're

supposed to hate the sea, remember? Everyone has been keeping secrets, but I can handle the *truth*!' His impatience and frustration had finally boiled over.

'Enough,' Ida barked. 'I've told you already, there are things that your parents—'

'Why were you disqualified after swimming the Channel?' he interrupted, silencing Ida in a second. She froze, the only sound the water splashing her ankles.

'I don't—' She faltered.

'I know that you're a swimmer, just like me. How could you not be? Living in a place like this . . . in a home like that! With the sea breeze rattling down the hallways, and Corallium water running through the pipes.'

Ida's skin reddened. 'Casper, I don't know what Beryl has been telling you, but—'

'She's barely told me anything! I've had to look for answers by myself.' He shifted his weight awkwardly between both feet, his webbed toes rippling with shame before the next sentence found its way to his lips. 'I've seen your trophies, and the coral paintings too. Your closet is filled with frames and ribbons; you were a *champion*!'

Ida's face fell. 'You've been snooping through my things?'

'I didn't mean to pry,' Casper answered quickly. His words were urgent. 'I thought, if it was about my own past, that I had a right to know. I hoped it might explain the reason I've been kept from Corallium.'

Ida softened, the stiffness in her body melting even as the frown stayed fixed upon her brow. 'So you found my trophies,' she said. 'That means you also—'

'Found the pictures,' Casper finished her sentence. 'I love Beryl like a second grandmother. Just because you broke up, it doesn't mean you can't be friends.'

'Oh, Casper,' Ida sighed, a sad smile twitching at the corner of her mouth. She looked out to sea where the sunrise was now an orb of orange hanging low on the horizon. 'It's more complicated than you realize. I know what it's like to burn for the sea. To long for the cold water on your limbs, and to wish that it would hold you in its grip.'

Casper's heart was full of affection for his grandmother, and he hung on every word. 'So why put yourself through it?' he asked gently. 'Why abandon the sea just because of the Channel Swimming Syndicate?'

'Because some things are bigger than us,' she said.

'What do you mean?'

Ida turned back. 'It must have been hard at home, with your parents so against your swimming. I'm afraid you've me to blame for their behaviour. When you finally arrived in Corallium I should've helped you make up for lost time. Instead, I asked you to stay on dry land like your dad. I was afraid, you see.'

Casper looked to Ida with a puzzled expression.

'Your parents were furious on the day I swam the Channel. They left Corallium soon after and I thought I'd never see you again. I thought that if I swore off swimming, removing the risk of another near miss, then in time they might forgive me.'

'Forgive you for what?' squawked Casper.

'Your webbed feet,' said Ida.

Casper froze and the world drained of colour. He felt exposed, like a single white spotlight was suddenly shining down on him. His toes throbbed.

'My webbed feet?' he blurted. 'How did you know?'

Ida stepped from the water and Casper looked down with a gasp. His grandmother fanned her toes, revealing her very own pair of enormous webbed feet

– larger and more brilliant even than Casper's.

'Everyone in my family has them,' she smiled. 'For as long as Corallium has been here, so has our family.'

Casper was lost for words.

'The pull you feel towards the sea every second of the day,' she continued. 'The fact that you sense a connection to this place, like it's a piece of your soul . . .'

'The visions of coral,' whispered Casper.

'Ah,' said Ida. 'You've even more intuition than I realized. Those images, your insatiable thirst for the sea, and your feet. They're all because of me, Casper. They're all because of Corallium.'

'So the stories *are* true,' whistled Casper.

'Yes, this was once the bottom of the sea. Our ancestors lived in the water, and the castle grew from the reef like a crown of coral. Over the centuries the sands shifted, the rock expanded, and the seabed was forced through the waves and into daylight. Now all that remains of that extraordinary time and place is the castle, a longing for the water . . .'

'And our feet.'

Casper was amazed. He'd never known anyone who had webbed feet like him. He'd been taught to keep them a secret for so long, even though they were his pride and joy.

But now he knew the truth.

They *were* a gift.

He followed his grandmother's example, kicking off the cumbersome shoes which choked his feet, and allowed his truest self to shine through for the first time ever.

'When I saw the shell mosaics I wasn't sure I could truly believe it,' smiled Casper, embracing the whole truth. He imagined swimming through the underwater grotto while a pair of large gills flapped in his neck.

'You've seen the shell grotto?' said Ida.

'Dev found a doorway near the castle. You *knew* it was there?'

'I've not been down since I sealed up the other entrance and buried it with bracken. The instruction to keep our heritage a secret from the world has been passed down through the generations, though the odd person slips up. They've been accused of witchcraft, or even worse. The truth has always been dangerous.

'I've never come so close to ruin than when I stood

on this very beach with the Channel Swimming Syndicate, disqualified. I was careless, and they saw my webbed feet. They didn't know the full story, but they kept my "abnormality" – their word – out of the newspapers . . . Even so, I couldn't risk it happening again.'

'And so you left Beryl,' said Casper knowingly.

'Yes,' choked Ida. 'She may not have webbings, but we certainly share an unquenchable love for the sea. How could we continue a life when I had to tear myself from the water? When she knew that I was keeping something secret? I locked up the beach hut and never went back.'

Casper reached up to place his hand on Ida's shoulder. 'But you couldn't stay away,' he said. 'With the sound of the waves drifting through your window, it would be impossible. You'd come down in the middle of the night, when nobody would see, and swim.'

'So now you know,' Ida said warmly. She took Casper's hand and walked him into the shallows, their feet embraced by the water. 'You know why I was disqualified from swimming, why you yearn for the water and why I've hidden myself away in the hope I'd be allowed back into your life.'

Ida reached inside the collar of her nightgown and pulled on a thick emerald ribbon.

'They never did ask for this back, though . . .'

The gold medallion, embellished with the merman logo of the Channel Swimming Syndicate, glinted in the rising sun.

'You did all of that, just to see me again?' asked Casper, his eyes wide.

'Of course!' Ida beamed. 'You're my grandson. I had to show your father our secret was safe. He was obsessed with the horror stories passed down by our ancestors. He'd never liked his webbed feet much, and when I slipped up, he reached breaking point.'

'*He* has webbed feet too?' Casper shook his head with the sudden realization.

'Oh, yes,' laughed Ida, before her face fell again. 'Your father feared the truth more than anyone, worried we'd all be thrown into some sterile lab for experiments. He couldn't even trust Beryl, and made me swear she'd never know.'

She sighed sadly.

'It must've been terribly hard for him to leave this place. Even regular folk feel a pull to the water, but it's near impossible for our family to ignore.

Being away has left a weight in your father's stomach which he blames me for. He grew resentful, thinking he was finally free of some kind of magic spell when in fact keeping this fundamental part of his identity pushed down was poisoning him from the inside out . . .'

Casper paused, counting the times his father had told him to keep his fleshy webbed feet hidden. Now, he could see that Roger Delmare had actually been fighting something in himself.

His heart swelled with empathy for his father.

'And that's everything,' Ida said. They swished their feet in the water, the large toes magnified by the early morning light on its surface. 'Now you understand why you can never swim the Channel.'

It took a few moments for Casper to register the words.

'What?' he breathed.

'If the Channel Swimming Syndicate learn of the advantage your webbed feet carry in the water, at best you'd be disqualified.'

'And worst?'

They stood in silence as the waves bashed against their shins with a cold slap. Casper felt his heart shatter – every hope and dream which had filled it for so long now slowly leaking like oil.

'I'm so sorry, Casper.'

He was overcome by a desire to dive head first into the waves and disappear, so that the tears welling behind his eyes might wash away with the tide.

Neither had the capacity in that moment to notice the bald old man who loitered quietly behind them, listening intently to the tail end of their conversation. He spat the straw from his mouth back into a cup filled with prune juice and smiled, his wrinkled lips stretching ever wider with excitement.

CHAPTER TWENTY-THREE

Red Meat and Webbed Feet

Casper had never wanted anything more than to be the youngest person to swim the English Channel. Now, his chance was in serious jeopardy, and all because of something outside of his control. All because of who he was, and how he'd been born.

Maybe there *was* a curse on the record after all . . .

Once she'd learnt of his training, Ida had encouraged Casper to abandon his swim rather than risk disqualification. But ultimately, she left the decision to him.

'I never should have asked you to make me that promise,' she'd said. 'The ocean runs through your veins, just as you've always suspected. Nothing will keep you from me or Corallium ever again, and it's time we let you make your own mistakes for a change.'

But *was* it a mistake?

Casper had been gifted with ten incredible toes for a reason. He was born for the water, and now that he knew it, why should he suffer just because he was different? It wasn't like he was actually *cheating*. He didn't want to be the fastest, or the greatest.

Just the youngest.

And when another young swimmer came along in a few years' time with a dream of breaking the record themselves, Casper would *not* be like Bernie.

Casper would welcome it.

He wasn't a merman, like the shell mosaics of his ancestors in the ancient grotto. He'd trained and trained for *weeks*, eating nothing but pasta and spending hours sitting inside the freezer drawer as blue as an icicle.

Casper had *worked* for this.

'I hope you know what you're doing,' Ida said the following morning, while Casper boiled a pan of tortellini. She looked fearful, her worry lines deep like canyons. 'Records don't mean all that much, really. Why don't we find a quiet patch of beach along the seafront and swim together?'

'I would love that,' smiled Casper. 'But I *need* to do this . . . I'm so close I can *taste* it! I've wanted this for too long, and I'm almost twelve—'

'Hello?' came a new voice, accompanied by a short rap on the front door.

'Come in,' Ida called, surprised by the visitor.

'I invited Wynn for breakfast; I hope that's OK,' said Casper, dolloping pasta into two large bowls. He placed them on the table as Wynn appeared in the hallway.

'Good morning,' she cheered, before seeing Ida. 'Yum, tortellini. Just what I need – the waves are out of control!'

'It's fine,' said Casper with a smile. 'Granny knows about my swimming. You don't need to pretend I'm watching you surf all day.'

'Well, that's a relief. It's like a millpond down there.'

'Perfect for swimming,' Ida sighed.

'Come with us.' Casper beamed at the thought. 'You and Beryl can train me together!'

Ida choked on a mouthful of breakfast, which for her was a pile of smoked kippers. 'I'm not quite ready for that . . . But you two eat up and get going. *If* you're really sure.'

Casper told Wynn everything on their short walk to the seafront. His grandmother's words seemed to whistle through the trees, like the birds were calling out with their family secret – so strange a feeling it was to finally know the truth.

Everything around them had once belonged to the sea.

'I knew there was something odd about your granny's front door,' said Wynn. 'The shell border was just like the grotto! It's all true, for real. Though it's a shame you can't breathe underwater – you might've saved yourself a few drownings.'

'At least I don't need to hide my feet from you any more,' said Casper. 'This whole time I've been digging them down in the sand.'

'Oh, I noticed. I just thought you must have hairy knuckles . . .'

Casper laughed deeply and broke into a run, desperate to get back in the water and tell Beryl everything too. The heather trail opened ahead, and he raced Wynn for the beach huts knowing his hero would be waiting.

But Beryl wasn't the only one.

The normally peaceful beach was swarming with people. Dozens of faces buzzed about the seafront, as if a nearby retirement home had smashed open on the sand like a beehive. It was busier than Casper had ever seen it.

The pair skidded down the dunes to meet Beryl.

'What's going on?' asked Wynn, breathless.

'A protest,' Beryl replied.

'About what?' Casper's stomach dropped like an anchor.

'There seems to be a fair bit of confusion over that.' Beryl indicated one of the placards which bounced past the beach huts.

'No red meat?' Casper whispered, reading the sign. The words were painted in large, angry letters, a stark contrast to the delicate lady who smiled while holding it high above her head. Her curls bounced in time to the rhythm of the crowd.

'Look at that one!' said Wynn, laughing.

Another protester sidled by in a cloud of sour perfume. Her placard read: *STEAK GAVE ME HIGH BLOOD PRESSURE*. It was followed closely by a third which declared: *IT'S TOO TOUGH TO CHEW!*

'It doesn't make a huge amount of sense,' Beryl chuckled. 'Then again, Bernie's sign is even stranger.'

'Bernie's?' asked Casper. He scanned the crowd of blue hair and silk scarves, looking for a flash of blonde. 'What does his say?'

'Something about webbed feet,' shrugged Beryl.

Bernie finally stepped into view through the parting crowd. He wore a yellow duckling onesie, a large hood covering his childish curls from the sun. A long orange beak at the front matched a pair of enormous plastic flippers on his feet . . .

Casper's body went numb.

He looked up to read the placard waving from Bernie's outstretched arm . . .

WEBBED FEET = CHEAT!

'There's the little fraudster,' he spat.

The whole crowd turned to look, while one elderly man towards the back used the distraction to stuff a fistful of beef jerky into his mouth.

'Oh, no,' said Casper. Wynn came to stand by his side.

'Oh, yes!' Bernie screeched. 'We've learnt all about your filthy little secret, and frankly we're disgusted. You thought you could swoop in here and steal my record by breaking the rules? Not today, sonny Jim!'

'Who's Jim?' mouthed Wynn with a smirk, while Bernie climbed the nearest sand dune. He placed a megaphone to his lips.

'Please, don't!' Casper shouted, his plea drowned by the baying crowd of pensioners.

'WHAT DO WE WANT?' Bernie cried.

'RED MEAT BANNED!' they answered.

'WHEN DO WE WANT IT?'

'NOW!'

'For pity's sake,' Bernie sighed, pinching the bridge of his nose. 'For the last time, we're protesting that lanky little cheat's *webbed feet*.'

'What are you on about, Bernie?' asked Beryl.

Bernie sneered. 'So you still don't know there's a swindler in your midst. Just like his no-good grand-mother, that boy. A chip off the old block! I should've known the moment I laid eyes on him . . . The rotten apple never falls far from the tree!'

'Casper is *not* a cheat!' Wynn insisted, defending her friend.

'It's all right,' said Casper, holding up the palms of his hands. He exhaled deeply. Finally he was about to let go of the secret which had weighed him down for so long. 'It's true.'

'You see?' Bernie bellowed. 'He admits it!'

The crowd cheered in triumph, while a lone voice echoed above the din: 'It's very bad to eat so much mince at his age.'

'Casper, what do you mean?' asked Beryl, wrapping an arm around his shoulder. 'You're no cheat. You've been in the sea every day for weeks, swimmin' up and down this coast like a blue-bottomed flying fish. You've done everything I've asked, and risen to the challenge every single time an' all.'

'But I've been hiding something,' Casper groaned. He kicked off his shoes and let his large feet flop to the sand where they sizzled in the warmth.

'This is me.' He shrugged, waiting for the imminent cries of disgust.

'Is that all?' asked Beryl, looking between Casper's toes and the protesters' placards.

'But—' spluttered Bernie. 'Look at those monstrosities!'

'The only monstrous thing is that baggy yellow onesie. As for Casper, he's worked his bum off getting ready for the Channel swim and a few flaps of skin don't change a thing.'

Casper's heart felt full.

'I hope you've not been stressing over feet,' said Beryl.

'I didn't want you thinking I was a weirdo, so I kept them a secret.'

'You see?' Bernie bellowed, waving his placard in the air. 'He admits it! Webbed feet equals cheat. He's a fraud, just like his deceitful grandmother.'

'Ida?' Beryl asked.

'Yes, *Ida*. Do you know any other charlatans knocking about in Corallium? At least she had the courtesy to shut herself away.'

'No,' shushed Beryl. 'I mean, *Ida*!'

Casper's granny had appeared on the sand with Triton nipping at her heels. 'What's going on? Why is Bertha Vale over there screaming about filet mignon?'

'Speak of the devil,' sneered Bernie. 'We were just discussing your grandson's abnormality.'

'Abnorma—' Ida frowned, the word stinging, before she noticed Casper's fleshy feet flapping in the breeze. 'I see.'

'And what do you have to say about it?' Bernie demanded.

Ida gave a shaky breath, lifted her chin and walked to stand beside Casper on the sand.

'This.'

She kicked off her own large shoes, which sailed across the beach in a curve of leather to land in a heap by the surf. Her enormous webbed toes wriggled gently.

'Good grief!' Bernie hollered.

'Now that feels *much* better.'

'Awesome,' whispered Wynn.

Ida smiled at Casper, whose own grin stretched impossibly wide.

'I'm sorry for ruining the family secret,' he said.

'There's not a jot to be sorry for. I should've done this a decade sooner.'

'Is this why?' asked Beryl, her eyes wet. 'The reason the Syndicate disqualified you? Why they called you a cheat?'

'I'm afraid so.' Ida hung her head.

'And it's the very *same* reason that Casper won't be breaking any records of his own!' taunted Bernie with a chuckle. He pulled a carton of apple juice from inside his onesie and stabbed a straw in the top. 'Mother has already spoken with the Channel Swimming Syndicate, informing them of this *situation*. The boy has been banned and his date to swim the Channel cancelled. My record stands to see another day.'

Casper's heart sank again, his biggest fear realized. The thought of swimming the Channel, and the chance to break Bernie's record, had been the only thing getting him through the last few years of thrashing about in ponds and fountains; the days spent grounded in his barren home.

'That record is the only thing you've *ever* cared about,' said Ida.

Casper felt a stab to his heart. He looked up, pain etched in every corner of his face before he realized that his granny was speaking to Bernie. She was looking at the old man with the utmost contempt.

'Who cares about some stupid record?' asked Wynn. 'I think Casper's feet are brilliant!'

'But I've held that record for sixty years!' Bernie

shouted in disbelief. 'It's one of the greatest sporting achievements in the history of Corallium!'

'As I've said before,' started Beryl, 'there are more important things in life than records and trophies. Like talent, and determination. Drive. Passion. Accomplishment. Casper has proved that he's got these things in spades, and the rest.'

Casper filled with love for his friends. His greatest fear hadn't come to pass in the slightest. Beryl, Wynn and Ida accepted him for exactly who he was. They loved him *because* of who he was, webbed feet and all.

'You're right,' said Ida, after a moment's pause. 'Official records don't matter one bit. I should've realized that a long time ago . . . And that's why Casper's going to swim the Channel anyway.'

Casper's toes rippled with the fear of false hope. 'I am?'

'You are,' said Beryl, joining Ida at her side. 'Today.'

'But he can't!' spluttered Bernie. 'There are rules and regulations! You can't just swim off into the world's busiest shipping channel on a whim. It goes against every official protocol in place!'

'To heck with protocols,' smiled Ida.

'But I don't . . . They won't . . . I mean . . . *Argh*!'

Bernie squeezed his juice box in fury and amber liquid shot from the end of his straw like a pistol. He threw his protest placard to the ground and stamped on it, before shoving his thumb in his mouth and sucking. He turned on his heel and sloped back through the protesters, all of whom had ignored the commotion to carry on shouting about the dangers of dentures and overcooked rump.

'Thanks for all having my back,' smiled Casper, bending down to scratch Triton's head as he yapped excitedly. 'It means the world, but Bernie's right! I can't swim the Channel now.'

'The conditions are perfect!' insisted Ida. 'Seize the day, I say.'

'But if Bernie's mother has called the Channel Swimming Syndicate, we've bigger problems than my swim not being official. We don't even have a boat!'

Ida's brow creased in thought while Wynn puffed out her cheeks in disappointment. Beryl stood to the side, her eyes sparkling as the most ingenious plan began to form.

'Oh yes we do.'

CHAPTER TWENTY-FOUR

Les Moules-Frites Set Free

'High tide is in half an hour,' urged Beryl. She was leaning over the railings of *Les Moules-Frites* as the china plates clanged against its hull. 'We have one shot to time this perfectly, or all we'll manage is to move the boat a few metres down the beach.'

Casper and Wynn were on the dunes below the bow, digging frantically with large plastic spades. Triton burrowed at their side, and chunks of hard sand flew past their shoulders while they hacked at the earth which kept the tugboat aloft.

'How will we know when it's ready to move?' asked Wynn.

'Trust us,' came Ida's voice from somewhere above. 'We'll make sure the weight is balanced perfectly. This old girl should slide down the slope and on to the water with seconds to spare. Just make sure you keep digging before the flood current comes in!'

'This would be quicker if you gave us a hand,' Wynn suggested grumpily.

'We're old ladies, kid!' squawked Beryl.

'Now that we're down here doing the dirty work she's a frail old lady. But when she's swimming the Channel . . .' Wynn rolled her eyes, making Casper laugh loudly.

On deck, Beryl was dragging a squidgy green armchair from inside her cottage to the bow of the boat where another one waited, beside a pile of pans and the clamshell coffee table piled high with books.

'What else can I do?' asked Ida. 'I could start bringing the plant pots down from the roof?'

'Don't you dare!' Beryl teased. 'They're my babies! I won't have them flying about while the boat crashes into the sea.'

'The begonia bush is doing well,' smiled Ida. She shuffled her webbed feet nervously. 'Thank you for doing this. You've been so good to Casper. He thinks the world of you, and now you're making his dreams come true – official record or not.'

'I knew that boy had the ocean in his soul,' answered Beryl. 'He belongs by the water – just like his granny, the Delmare Dolphin.'

Ida blushed. She turned back to the railing and looked out at the sea.

'I don't know how you managed to stay away,' continued Beryl. She took Ida's hand in hers. 'I always knew that you were special, but I had no idea . . . A daughter of Corallium!'

'I'm sorry I never told you. My whole life I've been taught to keep this part of me a secret, and even managed to pass the shame down through my family.'

'But not Casper.'

'No,' smiled Ida. 'After my disqualification, I knew I had to do what I could to be part of his life again. Even though I couldn't bear the thought of you down here, thinking I had cheated . . .'

'You've swum the world and have a closet full of

trophies to prove it,' said Beryl. 'You earnt those, not your feet. You worked for them, harder than anyone I've known, until Casper Delmare turned up outside my beach hut. Who cares what some trumped-up officials think? You know what's in your heart, and so do I.'

Ida felt a decade of burden lift from her shoulders as though the sea breeze was gently blowing it away. 'I'm sorry I couldn't trust you with the truth.'

'Say nothing more,' said Beryl. 'We've the rest of time to make up for it!'

Below the hull, Casper wiped his brow as the August sun continued to beat down. He would have given anything to turn and charge into the sea that very second, but if *Les Moules-Frites* didn't move, his chance to swim the Channel would be gone.

'This isn't working,' he huffed. The tips of his fingers throbbed from gripping the short wooden handle of his spade. *If only my hands were bigger.*

An idea came to him, and he threw the tool aside, rolled on his back and began to shovel the grassy sand with his bare webbed feet – clearing twice as much with every scoop.

'You couldn't have done that earlier?' laughed Wynn.

'We might have a new problem,' Ida called from the boat with a grim expression. Casper craned his neck to see where her eyes pointed and his feet froze in mid-air, a clump of sand in each one.

'Mum, Dad!' he gasped.

His parents were hobbling towards him along the seafront, still covered in white cotton bandages and each with a single silver crutch under one arm. Triton looked up from his digging and growled in their direction.

'Casper!' his dad bellowed, grimacing as each step sank his feet in the sand. 'You're coming home right this second.'

'What?'

'Do as your father says and get down from there,' said Mum. 'It looks dangerous!' She surveyed *Les Moules-Frites* with alarm.

'I'm sorry but I can't,' said Casper, surprising himself with confidence.

'You what?' his father choked. 'You *can't*? You'll do what you're told, now get—' His face faded from beetroot red to floury white as his eyes landed on his son's webbed feet, which pulsed in the sunlight for all the world to see.

'Casper—' he spluttered. '*Feet!*'

'Put those away this instant,' his mother howled, as if expecting Mrs Marsh to pop her head around Beryl's begonia bush at any second. 'Where are your shoes? Get them on *now* before anybody else—'

'No,' said Casper calmly.

'N-n-no?' his parents stammered.

'No. I'm done hiding my feet, and I'm done with worrying what anyone thinks of them. I'm done hiding *me*! My feet have always made me feel special. They helped me feel a connection to the water, even when you made it your mission to keep me as far away from here as possible. I knew I belonged with the sea, and I was right . . . even though you never told me a thing about our history!'

'Casper,' his father started, a hint of a warning in his voice, 'I'm not sure what your grandmother has told you—'

'The truth!' Ida called from *Les Moules-Frites*. Casper's dad looked up, just noticing the presence of his elderly mother. 'I told him everything. We may not have dorsal fins, gills or tentacles for hair, but we are special. Casper *is* special, and he belongs by the sea . . . We *all* do!' She stepped forward and flopped her toes over the side of the tugboat with a slap of the paint. They wriggled happily and Casper smiled, his heart swelling.

'Casper, this place does strange things to our family,' urged Dad. 'It burrows under your skin and fills your head with rubbish that doesn't make sense in the normal world.'

'Then the world needs to change,' said Casper. If he was going back to Bramble-in-the-Oaks then he would leave every last bit of shame and fear right here, on the beach in Corallium. 'Don't you feel it, Dad?'

'Feel what?' his father replied, sweat beading on his forehead with the question. He tugged the white bandage wrapped around his neck with an index finger. 'Goodness, it's hot down here.'

'I *know* you feel it,' Casper urged. 'Our whole family does! We were all born with that same call to the water; with a need to feel the ocean on our webbed—'

'Stop,' his father interrupted wearily, the anger in his voice diminished.

'Listen to it, Dad. I know you want to!'

'Roger, no,' his wife urged. 'Think of all that hard work you've done to suppress it!'

Casper's dad stood fixed on the spot, his bandaged body slowly sinking as each of his muscles unclenched for the first time in a decade. He closed his eyes, and to Casper it seemed like his father was unlocking a piece of himself which had been strangled inside, starved of oxygen for who knew how long.

'Do it, Dad,' he said with a thrill.

Roger breathed a deep sigh, sweat pouring from his forehead, and kicked his heavy shoes off with a sharp flick of each ankle. His hairy webbed feet were twice the size of Casper's, and he wagged them slowly, easing into the feeling of freedom for the first time in memory.

'They're brilliant!' cheered Casper.

His father half-smiled, as if unsure that he agreed with the appraisal . . . But a moment later, he was overcome by a feeling of completeness. Roger looked down to see that the tide had come in and the water was lapping at the tips of his toes . . .

'Wow,' he breathed.

Casper knew what his father was experiencing – a soothing sensation, running up through every limb as he was reunited with the missing part of himself.

'Thank you, son.'

Casper leapt down from the hull of the tugboat and took a running jump into his dad's arms.

'Ow!' howled Roger, his bandaged arms aching while Casper fell to the floor with a thump. They burst into laughter as Sophie looked on, holding her silver crutch tightly.

'Don't think for one second we'll be spending our savings on a whole new wardrobe of fancy shoes for you both,' she tutted.

'I don't mean to break up this incredibly weird family moment,' interrupted Wynn. 'But the tide is starting to recede.'

Casper looked to the ground and his heart fluttered with panic. Wynn was right. His dad's feet were already clear of the water, the ebb current drawing it slowly back out to sea. 'I don't think we're going to make it,' he said.

'Think again!'

Beryl stood proudly on the bow of *Les Moules-Frites*, a telephone in her hand. 'While you lot have been having your mothers' meeting, I was calling for reinforcements.'

She pointed along the beach. Dev was sitting on

the back of his yellow digger with Tan, waving wildly and trundling towards them. He wore a wide-brimmed summer hat which was tied with a big cream bow at the front.

'Yes, Dad!' bellowed Wynn, while Beryl and Ida whooped.

'What is going on?' asked Sophie, pointing at the tugboat. 'Why are you digging up this rusty old heap anyway?' Ida took the phone from Beryl's hand, preventing it from flying through the air at Sophie's head.

'I'm swimming the Channel!' said Casper.

'What, *now*?' his parents asked in disbelief, as Dev arrived and quickly rolled the digger up to the dunes.

'Love the hat, Dev,' Ida called.

'Thanks,' he laughed. 'You should've seen Elsie. She was absolutely green with envy.' He hopped down from the digger with a thump and his eyes landed on the large flippers of Casper and his dad. 'Are those . . .' he spluttered. 'I mean . . . your feet! They're just like the imprint I found inside the grotto.'

So he'd found it too, Casper thought.

'You were right all along, Dev,' said Ida, her voice laden with guilt. She appeared at Casper's side, her own set of webbed toes wriggling. 'The children of Corallium are real, just like you suspected, and my family's the living proof.'

Dev looked between the three pairs of feet and smiled. 'I've always hoped that I'd meet you one day, but I never would have guessed that you were right in front of my eyes!'

'I'm sorry we couldn't tell you,' continued Ida. 'I know that you've only ever had the best intentions, but history has shown that others aren't always so kind to those of us who are a little bit different.'

'I understand,' said Dev with a warm smile. 'Being an archaeologist is a unique experience . . . We sift through layers of time in the form of sand and soil, hoping to uncover the stories which have fallen into myth. But you, I mean . . . look at you! History in human form.'

Casper beamed, and Ida placed an arm around his shoulder with a squeeze. Dev hopped back on the digger and planted his sun hat on top of Tan's head. He turned on the machine and raised his voice above the engine. 'Now, everyone who is coming to France – on board right away! This won't take long.'

'Quick!' said Casper. He ushered his parents up

the sandy slope to *Les Moules-Frites*, each of them wincing with pain while their bandages blew in the breeze like badly wrapped Egyptian mummies.

Wynn abandoned her spade and slid down from the hull with Triton in her arms, joining them at the wooden plank walkway. They were only just across when Dev's digger took a chunk from the earth below and the whole boat groaned. The ebbing tide ran back into the hole which had been left by the digger. Water pooled at the base of the hull.

'Just one more should do it,' Dev called from the controls. 'The sand will collapse below you and create a slipway on to the water.'

'Everyone to the bow,' instructed Beryl. She pulled the plank on deck and ran forward. 'We've got to get the weight right. Gird your loins!'

The group rushed to the front of the ship and lent their bodies to the cause.

Dev moved the digger into position.

'Ready in three . . .'

Ida grabbed the railings with one hand and Beryl's with the other. Together they braced for impact.

'Two . . .'

Roger and Sophie collapsed into the green armchairs, their bandaged limbs aching as they realized what was about to happen.

'One...'

Casper and Wynn grinned wide, clutching Triton tightly. They leant forward, like two wooden figureheads mounted to the bow of a grand pirate ship.

'Now!'

Dev took another mammoth chunk of sand from beneath the hull of Beryl's tugboat and a deluge of water flooded into the hole left behind.

The dune gave way.

With a huge groan, *Les Moules-Frites* tipped on its axis and began to crash from its perch, pulling huge stalks of ancient grass from the root and sending a tidal wave of sand down the beach as it hurtled towards the water. China plates rattled violently against the hull with the sound of chattering teeth.

The boat skidded through the foaming surf, firing spluttering white fireworks of water all around like a sprinkler. Its enormous weight carried it forward with the speed of a runaway jet ski and finally, it was afloat on the sea.

Les Moules-Frites was free.

CHAPTER TWENTY-FIVE

The Corallium Strait

Casper stood on the beach in a red swimming cap, his body heavy with goose fat and glistening like a piece of uncooked meat. The water lapped at his large webbed toes, which were fanned proudly and flapping in the wet sand with hope and excitement.

In the near distance, *Les Moules-Frites* bobbed elegantly on the waves as though she had never left the sea's beloved hold. The engine purred softly, waiting for Casper to walk into the water, ready to escort him on the journey across the narrow sea to France. Casper could see Wynn on board, waving frantically from the stern and cheering inaudibly while her father and brother stood beside her. Behind, at the bow of the boat, were the fuzzy shapes of his parents still clinging to their armchairs which slid about the deck in time with the swell of the sea.

Inside the small cottage Casper's two heroes manned the vessel. His Granny Ida stood at the helm, her grip strong on the wheel, while Beryl the Bazooka ransacked the cupboards for every banana, protein bar, high-carb drink and bottle of water she could find. She threw them to the floor in a heap of untapped stamina – every little thing that might help to keep Casper's energy up while swimming the Channel.

This was it.

It no longer mattered whether the record was official or not. Casper had worked towards this moment for such a long time. Every fountain flutter kick, and the long sessions spent in Mrs Marsh's garden pond . . . The countless hours of watching Beryl's news report on the battered tape in his sock drawer . . .

It had all been worth it, and more, for this moment.

He knelt down to run his fingers through the sea foam as the water invited him forward.

'Casper?'

He turned with surprise at the voice to find several familiar faces: Sheila, the salon owner, and Vera the librarian. Wilbur, from the funicular office; Dev's bingo rival, Elsie; and Mabel, whom Casper had seen leading a charge of extraordinary women on runs around the town.

'We wanted to be here to see you off,' said Vera.

'What do you mean?' asked Casper. He stood up, instinctively burrowing his feet in the sand before shaking off the desire to hide them. Instead, he fanned his toes proudly.

'That's quite the set of fins,' smiled Mabel, the cuffs on her flowery swimsuit tickling her wrists.

'Thanks.'

'We heard about Bernie's protest,' said Sheila. 'I'm sorry we weren't there to back you up, but we'd all been told it was something to do with red meat—'

'They'll have to tear the sirloin from my cold dead hands!' cried Wilbur.

'Yes, we know,' tutted Sheila, her bouffant hair shaking with her head.

'Back me up?' asked Casper, wondering what that meant before quickly seeing that he wouldn't need an answer.

Each of them had slipped off a pair of large shoes to reveal their own set of flabby webbed feet – every toe a different size and shape, but all of them joined together by a fleshy spade of webbing.

'You're all like me,' stuttered Casper.

'Yes, and there are plenty more of us too,' said Elsie, the pink belt from Dev's fluffy dressing gown wrapped around her neck. 'A very long time ago our people went their separate ways, for safety, but—'

'The children of Corallium *always* find their way home,' finished Mabel.

'It's hard to ignore that thirst for the water,' said Vera, her wide eyes still magnified by a gigantic pair of glasses. 'It can almost seem unquenchable at times, which I'm sure you know something about.'

Casper nodded, the knot in his stomach squirming even now with the sea lapping at his heels. Mabel stood beside him and swirled her toes in the surf. 'Nothing can beat this feeling for people like us. The water courses through our veins.'

'It's in our blood,' said Wilbur, his white ear hair wafting in the breeze.

'In our bones too,' added Sheila. 'And we hope that you know you're not alone.'

Casper looked towards *Les Moules-Frites* and saw his friends' beaming faces. 'I've never felt less alone in my whole life.'

'Get on with it!' Wynn's voice carried on the wind, and Casper laughed.

'You'd better listen to your friend,' said Elsie. 'She's sassy, that one. Just like her father.'

'Good luck,' said Mabel.

Casper smiled and stepped forward, the water rushing across his feet with a welcome home. Quickly he waded deeper into the sea – his skin prickling with a gentle reminder of the cold being kept at bay by the goose fat coating his body.

Suddenly the water was up to his chest.

Casper turned to see the strange group walking slowly back along the beach, waving encouragement as they went. High above them he could see pink fingers of coral creeping up through the woodland canopy, reaching towards the town where white sails billowed at the windows of every house like an armada of the sky.

The spirit of Corallium swelled inside him.

Casper took one last look at the rainbow Pride flag billowing high above the stern of *Les Moules-Frites*, snapped his goggles down and dove head first into the water.

High above the seafront, Agatha sat on a small balcony which jutted from the forehead of her home. Perched on her scooter with a tiny glass of amber sherry and another fat bag of prunes, her piercing eyes scanned the scene below while she waited. Finally they narrowed, landing on the bright yellow outline of her son.

Bernie was lumbering his way up one of the woodland paths, huffing and puffing with each step. When he approached the front door, Agatha drove back into the sweltering living room – its thick velvet curtains pulled shut on the August sun. The fireplace roared with an unseasonably scorching hot blaze.

'And?' said Agatha, the moment her son entered the lounge.

Bernie collapsed into his favourite armchair, his

face covered in sweat from climbing the path in his yellow duckling onesie. 'You should have seen him,' he smiled uncertainly. 'When I told the boy he'd been disqualified from swimming the Channel, I could swear I saw the exact moment his heart broke in two.'

Agatha sipped her sherry with a sneer and smacked her lips in satisfaction. This was what she lived for – protecting her family's legacy and crushing people's dreams. The fact that the two often went together, hand in hand, was a delicious bonus.

'And you'll never believe it,' Bernie continued, his breathless energy betraying the nerves beneath. 'That old fraud, Ida Delmare, has only got her own ungodly set of webbed feet as well!'

'You're joking,' Agatha grimaced.

'They both had them out for all the world to see! Four ripe, horrible flippers slapping about on the sand like wet fish. Vile.'

'So, that's why the Dolphin was disqualified *too*. It's quite poetic, don't you think?' Agatha raised her sherry in a mock toast, and Bernie nodded his head with relief.

He'd done it.

His official record would live to see another day, and that was all that mattered. That was what would make his mother proud ...

'I wish you had been there,' he smiled. 'You'd have loved every second! The humiliation, the *anguish*! And then the ridiculous sight of them trying to launch that junkyard of a ship on to the water.'

'What are you talking about?' asked his mother.

'*Lez Mooley Freet*,' said Bernie. 'That rusty eyesore that Beryl calls a home.'

'They launched *Les Moules-Frites*?' The vein in Agatha's neck began to throb as her ancient heart pumped rapidly – though still half the speed of a regular human being. 'Why are you only just telling me this? *Where* are they taking that ship?!'

'Um—' Bernie stuttered. 'It was those old hags. They convinced the boy! They said that records didn't matter,' he scoffed. 'They said to swim the Channel anyway.'

'WHAT?'

'Mother, it's fine. He's been banned by the CSS – you saw to that yourself. Even if the little rat makes it to France, it will never be official! It's a total waste of time.'

Agatha zoomed back towards the balcony, snatching a pair of binoculars from the bookcase as she passed. She crashed out into the scorching summer air, shivering from the sudden drop in temperature, and held the eyeglasses up to her face . . .

There it was. *Les Moules-Frites*. It bobbed on the waves about a kilometre from the shore like a battered bathtub toy. In the water, just beside it, was a small smudge of pink in a red latex cap.

He was swimming strongly.

'That little *twit* is already in the Corallium Strait!' shrieked Agatha, incandescent with rage. Bernie appeared on the balcony, his yellow tail wagging between his legs.

'I don't see what the problem is,' he squeaked.

'The *problem* is that twerp is about to swim the Channel,' spat Agatha. 'Your hard-earned record has never *been* at such great risk. Not for sixty years!'

'But he's banned, Mother,' reasoned Bernie. 'The Channel Swimming Syndicate know all about those awful feet. The "curse" has worked its magic, as always. There's no way that any swim by that cheat will be recognized, whether he finishes or not.'

'You fool,' hissed Agatha, her voice rough like

grated bone. 'What will people say once they hear that he did it? They won't care about the paperwork. All they'll know is that the legendary Beryl the Bazooka trained an eleven-year-old boy to swim the Channel. They won't give two hoots whether it's official or not!'

'But the record,' insisted Bernie. He tugged down the collar of his onesie and pulled the fat gold medal from inside. 'The boy will never have one of these! It will still be my name in the history books tomorrow morning and that's what matters. Isn't that what you've always said?'

'I said that *your* record is the only thing *you've* ever done that mattered.'

'But . . .' Bernie stumbled, scratching his blonde head.

'People will know. *We* will know that Casper Delmare made the crossing. *We* will know that your record is meaningless and that you've nothing left to show for yourself!'

Bernie slumped into the balcony's wicker seat. He felt his mother's cruelty lash him like a whip, her tongue sharp and drenched in poison. She stung him with every word.

'Whether that boy has an official record or not makes no difference. If he gets to France then *he* will be the youngest person to ever swim the Channel.'

'Well, then,' sighed Bernie, looking up to her as if for the first time. 'What should we do?'

Agatha stood from her scooter unsteadily and walked to the balcony's edge.

'We follow,' she scowled, looking out towards *Les Moules-Frites* which was slowly disappearing on the horizon. 'We make sure that Casper Delmare fails, at all costs.'

CHAPTER TWENTY-SIX

Sabotage in the South-West Shipping Lane

*I*n the middle of the sea, *Les Moules-Frites* was rocking furiously. With the engine barely running, the small boat was at the mercy of the waves which rose and fell like the stomach of a snoring giant – the bow dropping into a nosedive on every exhale.

'I'm going to be sick,' said Casper's pale-faced

father, still clutching an armchair and sitting next to his wife. 'Give me your handbag!'

Sophie pulled her purse down from one shoulder but before she could pass it, her own skin turned a woozy shade of green and she threw her face deep into its leather – disappearing with a gurgle.

'Got it!' cheered Wynn, catching a terracotta pot as it slid from Beryl's roof garden and landed in her arms. She was charging desperately about the deck with Ida and Tan, each of them helping to stop household items from flying overboard. Dev manned the helm inside.

'There's a china plate with a picture of Calypso about to go on the port side,' Beryl called from her perch atop the chimney pipe, where she sat like a pirate in a crow's nest.

'I'm on it!' called Wynn. She ran to the railings and leant over, catching the ornament in her fingertips as it fell loose of its hook and tumbled towards the sea.

'Good save!' cheered Beryl. 'Be a doll and bring up the rest, or before long we'll be leavin' a trail of antique crockery behind us.'

'You'd think we were her crew,' muttered Tan.

'For the next eight hours we are,' said Wynn, stooping to collect the next plate.

Other ornaments, furniture and a barrel of goose fat continued to slide up and down the wooden deck while Triton happily chased them.

'Teapot!' Beryl yelled from her roost.

'I'll save it,' called Ida, running inside the cottage and finding it safely behind the glass cupboard doors. 'Beryl, the teapot is fine.'

'I know, but get the kettle on, will you?' she shouted back.

Ida tutted, peering back inside the cottage. 'I might need a hand in here, you know.' The rest of Beryl's kitchen utensils were rolling back and forth on the floor of the sitting room, like loose change in an otherwise empty drawer.

'We can sort the mess later,' Beryl shouted back.

A loud *CLUNK* echoed from somewhere below deck.

'That'll be my wardrobe.'

Casper was face down in the water, listening to the hubbub on deck with a secret smile. The south-west shipping lane was firmly in his sights and the first large cargo vessels loomed on the horizon, growing larger with every mounting wave.

He felt good.

His arms cut through the choppy water like a scythe, pulling him forward with every rotation while his faithful webbed feet churned behind.

Casper had been swimming for more than three hours, and Corallium seemed impossibly far behind. Regardless, he felt more at home here in the middle of the sea than he had for a single day in Bramble-in-the-Oaks.

The surface was crystal clear, and sank away into a misty blue haze. The thought of unseen creatures swimming on the seabed, one hundred metres or more beneath his wriggling feet, prickled his skin with another cold ripple. He imagined the Channel Tunnel winding its way through the rock even further down, and the passengers inside the speeding trains on their way to a plate of pink macarons or a night at the Paris opera.

'Casper, feedin' time!'

Beryl's voice gurgled in his ears. He looked up through his goggles to see a bright sports bottle land in the water ahead. Casper swam forward, stuck the nozzle between his teeth and sucked the warm energy drink into his mouth. His salty tongue screamed with relief and the sugar coursed through his body finding every limb. His webbed feet pulsed with renewed strength. He threw himself back into the navy sea, picking up his stroke as if he'd never come to a standstill at all.

The bottle rolled on the surface before a sharp tug pulled it backwards through the waves towards *Les Moules-Frites*.

Beryl held the end of a string and reeled the bottle in like a flapping fish. 'Casper's looking good,' she beamed proudly.

'He's had one heck of a coach,' replied Ida. 'Thank you for making this happen.'

'It's been a pleasure,' said Beryl. 'It turns out that you Delmares really do belong in the water.' They smiled, before an unpleasant retch turned their attention to the bow.

'Are we in France yet?' grumbled Roger, his face greener than the armchair he hugged. He wrestled Sophie for control of the handbag while Triton sat by their feet, unravelling a bandage with his teeth.

'Just a few more hours until we cross the separation zone,' said Ida. 'Then we'll enter the north-east shipping lane and finally reach French inshore waters.'

'Translation – not for another six hours, at least,' added Beryl.

Casper's parents groaned together, and Roger finally seized control of the handbag, throwing his face inside with a heave.

'Are you sure he's a Delmare?' Beryl asked through the side of her mouth.

'He's got the webbed feet all right,' laughed Ida. 'But maybe not the sea legs.'

One nautical mile behind them, Baby Face Bernie and his mother sat aboard a speedboat which bounced across the waves like a bright red skimming stone. At the stern, Bernie held a straw hat in one hand and the boat's tiller with the other. His body juddered under the strain of holding it steady, controlling the rudder's direction. Agatha sat in the bow, her clawing hands on the wood like the talons of a carved vulture mounted on the prow to scare off would-be pirates.

'Faster!' she screeched over the roaring sound of

the engine. Her delicate hair blew wildly, threatening to fly away with a wave goodbye to her scalp.

'I'm going as fast as I can,' said Bernie, tugging his stripy blue swimsuit which would've looked at home on a Victorian ten-year-old. 'Any faster and the engine might give out, leaving us stranded here in the Channel.'

'Rather stranded at sea than return to Corallium a failure,' hissed Agatha. 'Now, go faster . . . FASTER, I SAID!' She raised an oar from the floor of the boat and hit Bernie across the side of the head.

'Whatever you say,' he squeaked, rubbing a cheek. He pulled the throttle and the boat sped up, shaking violently from the strain. It thumped on the water after every wave, and Bernie gave a nervous whimper.

'You snivelling old fool,' his mother jeered. 'Don't you realize that this is all for you? Just look at the lengths I've gone to protect your reputation; to save you from the shame of that pre-teen twit besting your achievement!'

Bernie sniffed sadly. 'I was a pre-teen twit once too, you know. I was only a little older than Casper on the day I made you the *proudest mother on earth*!' The words felt hollow in his mouth, and more meaningless than ever.

'Well, imagine how *proud* I'll be when you let that record slip through your bony fingers,' sneered Agatha. 'If that web-footed freak reaches France, it will be as if your swim never happened; as if you were never even *here*!'

Bernie sank into his seat, more bruised by his mother's cruelty than he'd ever thought possible. He'd spent his whole life trying to preserve her pride, and now he wasn't sure she'd actually been proud of him to begin with.

The pair continued to crash through the water in silence, their bottoms bumping on their seats with each slap of a wave. The speedboat rudder vibrated up through the tiller and into Bernie's arm, juddering a warning which went bone deep.

Suddenly a loud *caw* echoed above the sound of the engine's aggressive hum. Bernie looked to the sky and saw a lone seagull, flying overhead. It swooped low and before he could call out a warning the bird had landed a wet, white dropping on Agatha's head with a squelch.

'WHAT THE—'

'It's meant to be good luck, Mother!' Bernie cheered, attempting to buoy her spirits. Perhaps it signalled that their mission would be a success?

'Well, it means a world of *bad* luck for that snivelling rat with wings!' she screeched. Agatha leant down, pulled a shiny flare gun from beneath her seat and turned it towards the sky. She aimed directly at the bird with a furious glare.

BANG!

A bright red spark flew high above them, missing the bird by centimetres. It zoomed past the creature's white feathers and exploded into a ball of light that hovered in the sky.

'What on earth was that?' asked Ida. The bang of the flare gun had carried all the way to *Les Moules-Frites*, and everyone on deck (who wasn't being sick into a handbag) scurried to the stern of the boat.

'It's a signal!' said Wynn, pointing to the bright flare floating overhead.

'There's a speedboat a few hundred metres behind,' called Dev from the door of the cottage, a pair of black binoculars pressed to his eyes. 'Shall we turn back and check it out?'

'We should,' frowned Ida.

'But we can't take Casper off course!' protested Wynn.

Tan rolled his eyes. 'He's disqualified anyway, what does it matter?'

'Maybe if Casper makes it to France the Channel Swimming Syndicate will reconsider. We've followed every single rule so far, we have to try.'

'*Please* no detours!' shouted Casper's mother breathlessly, swaying in her armchair with a grimace.

'We can't ignore a distress call,' insisted Beryl. 'Casper wouldn't want us to.'

'You're right,' agreed Ida. Tan gave his sister a satisfied smirk.

'But the record!' she insisted.

'There's no need,' Dev called again – back at the helm. 'The flare must have misfired; that speedboat is coming up fast . . . Really fast, actually. It's right on our tail.'

'*Les Moules-Frites*, dead ahead!' yelled Bernie.

'Excellent,' smiled Agatha, still clutching the cold flare gun in her skeletal fist. She scanned the deck with her hawk-like eyes, counting the bodies on board and searching for the thing she needed to finish this . . .

Ah ha!

The large barrel of goose fat, still sliding up and down the tugboat deck, uncovered and asking for trouble.

'Here,' she said, holding the flare gun out for her son.

'What are you doing?' asked Bernie.

'Giving you the chance to make things right. Take the flare gun and end it once and for all. We'll say it was an accidental discharge, with no one to blame but the faulty equipment. Just like Irene Ingleby . . .'

'What? I— Irene?' Bernie trembled, causing the boat to jerk awkwardly on the water. Agatha faltered but quickly regained her seat on the bow, still holding the gun towards her son with the offer of sabotage. 'No. I won't do it!'

He shook his head stiffly.

'Fine,' spat Agatha. 'I'll do it myself!' She snapped her fingers around the grip and turned to face the copper tugboat, which grew closer by the second.

'Mother . . .'

She lifted the flare gun in her fist and pointed it towards *Les Moules-Frites*, aiming straight for her target.

'Agatha! What are you *doing*?' screamed Beryl, the

two boats now just a few lengths apart. 'Are you really so desperate to keep some lousy record that you'd put *all* our lives in danger?'

'Oh, no,' Agatha smiled, her purple eyes raging. 'Just yours.'

'NO!' yelled Bernie. He lunged at his mother, grabbing hold of her arm and wrestling her furiously for control of the flare gun.

'Get off me, you old fool!'

'I won't let you do this,' choked Bernie, his eyes wet while his scrawny limbs attempted to free the weapon from her alarmingly strong grip.

'Listen to your son, Agatha,' Ida called.

'It's Irene Ingleby all over again,' Wynn cried above the noise of the struggle.

'Who?' said Tan with a confused pout.

'Irene!' yelped Bernie, caught off guard by the name. His grip on the flare gun slackened and Agatha seized her moment, wrenching her hand free. She pushed her son back to the stern of the boat with a crash.

'Everyone, get down!' shouted Dev, charging from the cottage. He grabbed Wynn and Tan by their collars and pulled them both to the deck.

Ida and Beryl crouched below the railings, their eyes squeezed shut as they held Triton close and braced themselves for what might be coming. Roger and Sophie fell back into their armchairs – too distracted by nausea to properly understand what was going on.

Agatha raised the flare gun.

She looked down the barrel, found the open tub of fat in its sight . . .

And took aim at *Les Moules-Frites*.

CHAPTER TWENTY-SEVEN

The Separation Zone

Casper bobbed in the water, happy to notice the swell subsiding as he made his way into the separation zone. Was he really halfway across the Channel? The feeling of being so far from land in either direction thrilled him, and he smiled, allowing a large glug of seawater to rush inside his mouth.

He sat up, coughing and spitting from the horrible taste, and looked about for Beryl – hoping another feed would wash the salt from his tongue, but . . .

The tugboat was gone.

He spun in the water and saw that *Les Moules-Frites* had fallen way behind him. A small speedboat bobbed off its port side.

Baby Face Bernie flopped about by the rudder, his straw hat floating away on the water, and at the bow of the speedboat his ancient mother pointed a flare gun directly at Casper's friends.

'No!' he screamed across the waves.

Agatha's eyes followed the voice and Casper felt the familiar cold creep down his spine. Her sharp, hypnotic stare found him. Her body tensed and twisted. Her determined face melted into a picture of fury.

'You,' she raged.

The flare gun in the ancient crone's hand left its mark aboard *Les Moules-Frites* and swivelled. Agatha stood on two shaky legs and took fresh aim, directly at the boy in the water.

Casper's blood turned to ice, the goose fat lathering his body unable to protect him from the arctic chill that now swaddled his heart like a frosty glove. He kept his eyes focused on Agatha, ready to try and deeply duck below the water at the last second.

His heart was racing.

Agatha held a finger to the trigger, and then . . .

She was floored.

Bernie had charged at his mother's knees, knocking her forward. The flare gun went off in her hands and fired into the water with a pathetic fizz, before the gun itself flew from Agatha's grip.

Splosh.

It was gone. The two of them fell into the bow of the speedboat with a heavy thud, and their combined weight tipped the vessel's nose into the sea.

'Look what you've done!' shrieked Agatha.

Water flooded over the bow and into the boat, filling it in seconds. They scrambled back to the stern, but it was too late for the boat, now heavy with seawater, to right itself. They were sinking quickly.

Casper didn't pause for a moment.

He threw his face back into the water and swam towards them, so fast that he might've been a shot from Agatha's flare gun himself.

'Let them drown!' Wynn yelled from *Les Moules-Frites*. Her father tapped her lightly on the head in reproach. 'I was only kidding,' she frowned. 'But Agatha *did* just try and sink our boat in the middle of the Channel.'

Casper reached the flooded speedboat in seconds and found the sorry pair floating fully in the water. Bernie looked down to see the deck sink towards the depths beneath their feet like the ghost of his mother's wicked plan.

Casper took Bernie's arm and draped it over one shoulder, before reaching for Agatha—

'Don't you *touch* me!' she cawed.

Her head dipped below the surface, her next words swallowed in a stream of bubbles which rose from her mouth to burst on the waves.

'Oh, shut up, Mother,' said Bernie.

He grabbed her by the collar and lifted her slowly to the surface like a wet dog, where she continued to grumble in between gasps for air. Casper kicked his webbed feet, slowly dragging the two of them towards the safety of *Les Moules-Frites*.

A short while later they lay on deck, panting with exhaustion. Beryl handed around mugs of hot tea and small stacks of sugary shortbread, while Agatha seethed from her seat in one of the armchairs.

'I'm so proud of you, Casper,' said Ida. 'You were

swimming so brilliantly, yet you sacrificed any chance of crossing the Channel by turning back to rescue these two idiots. You're an absolute hero.'

'But can't you just carry on?' asked Roger optimistically. He and his wife had finally broken through their nausea and joined the group beside Beryl's cottage. 'You made it this far, why not finish it off?'

'I can't,' said Casper. 'My swim was over the moment I helped Bernie and his mum. You can't touch another person for the whole swim, let alone a boat. So now I'm on board *Les Moules-Frites*, I'm doubly disqualified!'

'It's just so unfair,' said Wynn. 'You were saving lives, it's not like you were—'

'Caught in a mackerel net?' asked Tan with a huff. He crossed the deck to sit in the shade of Beryl's cottage with his tea.

'You know that's not what I meant,' said Wynn sincerely.

Beryl sighed deeply. 'Every kid who's tried in six decades has been disqualified, or worse. If there was any hope of those bureaucrats at the Channel Swimming Syndicate giving Casper's webbed feet a pass, too many other rules have been broken now too.'

'And that's all that matters!' cackled Agatha. Her cold laugh was punctuated by a wet coughing fit as she brought the sea up from inside her lungs. 'Bernie's record lives to see another day. The *curse* has seen to that.'

'Don't you mean your sixty years' worth of work?' said Casper.

Agatha snarled. 'What?'

'From the moment I arrived in Corallium, people have said to give up. They've told me that my hard work was all for nothing, because the "curse" of the Channel-swimming children would stop me in my tracks...'

Wynn looked sheepishly from left to right and whistled awkwardly, but Casper threw her a warm smile.

'No one my age has made it as far as France since Baby Face Bernie,' he continued. 'They've had their hair chewed up by propellors, insulted the pastry-loving population of Paris, and even caught pneumonia from coating their body in Vaseline!'

'That reminds me,' interrupted Dev, adjusting his summer hat. 'I must add some Trésor de la Mer face cream to the weekly shopping list.'

Agatha ignored the distraction. 'And what about it?' she yelled. 'My son's record-breaking swim has bested each one of those wannabes. Every single imposter has failed, while he *alone* succeeded!'

'Mother—' started Bernie. His blonde hair somehow seemed askew. It dripped salty water down his forehead on to the gold medal of the Channel Swimming Syndicate which hung around his neck.

'Curse or no curse,' Agatha ignored him, 'Bernie's record stands!'

'Yes, it does,' agreed Casper, getting to his webbed feet and walking across the deck with a slap on each step. 'But not because of the curse.'

Casper reached up and grabbed Bernie's blonde fringe, pulling it gently as the sodden mop slid forward to reveal a bald and itchy-looking scalp.

Instantly, 'Baby Face' Bernie looked his age.

CHAPTER TWENTY-EIGHT

For the Record

'*Y*ou!' said Wynn, her face a picture of under-standing. 'You're the skipper from the pilot boat that chewed up Jeremy's mullet; the bald man who *pushed* a woman from a cruise ship, just to distract Julia Bellwether from her swim, and—'

'You're the deckhand from the fishing trawler,' finished Tan, standing up from the floor with a look of pure resentment. 'You're the reason I was caught by that mackerel net. It's because of *you* I was disqualified!'

'How could you do this?' asked Dev, his eyes on Bernie – furious.

'Bernie has made sure that no one finished this crossing for six decades,' said Casper. 'He's still doing it now! That adder couldn't find its way inside my granny's cupboard without assistance . . . He even stole a shark!'

'But how did you find the grotto?' asked Wynn. 'When we saw that double spiral drawn in the sand, I was sure it meant the curse was real – that it was somehow connected with Corallium.'

Bernie frowned, red-faced. 'Grotto? I have no idea what you're talking about.'

'I do,' said Tan.

Wynn and Casper gasped.

'I'm sorry,' he croaked to Casper. 'I've been watching you train. I guess I've been jealous – that you were planning to swim the Channel, and that you still enjoyed the sea in a way that I haven't since . . . well. When I saw that jet ski crash down the seafront, I thought if I drew the grotto's spiral in the sand it might scare you off. I knew Wynn had told you about the curse, and I hoped it might be enough to stop you.'

'See!' jeered Agatha. 'It was the boy all along.'

'No, I promise,' Tan insisted. 'I had no idea there was an adder in that cupboard, or goose fat in your sun cream bottle or any of the other stuff. When I saw that rowboat from the cliffs and then a *shark* in the water, I almost fainted. I'm sorry for trying to frighten you, but seeing you train for something I wanted so badly . . .'

'Don't worry,' said Casper, his heart full of empathy for Tan. 'It was all Bernie. He's been hiding in plain sight all along, wearing lumpy cardigans and letting his sore scalp breathe while he sucked on prune juice.'

'How long have you known?' Wynn asked, impressed.

'I've had my suspicions since we found those photos in the paper, but today . . . it's felt like history repeating.'

'The flare gun,' nodded Wynn in understanding.

'Bernie was on board Irene Ingleby's pilot boat sixty years ago, two weeks after his own successful swim across the Channel. He fired the flare gun that caused her boat to sink.' Casper turned to Bernie with a stern look. 'You would've killed your friend, just to keep a lousy record?'

'No!' yelled Bernie, taking Casper aback. 'I wouldn't.'

Triton snatched the blonde wig from Casper's hand, and charged down the deck with it swinging from his jaw. Bernie paced back and forth, his mother's eyes upon him.

'I'll admit to the rest, yes. For years I've tried my best to cling to that wretched record. It's the only worthwhile thing I've ever done, or so my mother likes to tell me—'

'Quiet, you fool!' howled Agatha.

'I've stayed eleven years old for more than sixty years in the hope I could bottle that feeling... Accuse me of vanity and pride all you like, but I would have never done anything to put Irene in danger.'

'But you were on the boat,' frowned Casper. The mystery had come together in his mind like a jigsaw puzzle, but this piece didn't seem to fit. 'You were part of Irene's team. You pulled her from the sea when she was knocked out by the explosion.'

'Exactly,' said Bernie. 'I saved her! Irene was my

friend, and if someone was going to beat my record so soon I would have been glad it was her.'

'But if it wasn't you, then—' Casper's eyes swivelled across the deck to the sneering face of Agatha. 'You set that flare off! You caused the explosion that ripped through Irene's support boat and tried to do the same today, with *Les Moules-Frites*!'

'Someone had to stop that girl,' scorned Agatha. 'Bernie had barely held the record for a *fortnight*, but I was expected to sit back and let some little brat take it?'

'You put everyone on board that boat in danger, including your son!' said Beryl.

'And I'd do it again, if it meant protecting the one decent thing he ever did with his miserable life.'

'That's really all that matters to you?' asked Ida, sadness in her voice. She reached inside the collar of her blouse and lifted out the gold medal on its emerald ribbon. 'I was almost like you . . . I was so embarrassed to be disqualified when I swam the Channel, and all because of some skin between my toes. I thought that hiding myself away was the safest thing, but now I know that none of the people who matter would've given two hoots. It all means nothing if the same people that celebrate your victories tear you down when you fail.'

'Oh, please,' hissed Agatha.

'She's right,' said Bernie, taking his own medallion in one hand. 'I've spent my whole life keeping hold of that one moment in time. I thought it made you happy, but it never made me happy. *I don't even like swimming!* I wish I'd never stepped foot in the English Channel.'

'So that you could be even more pathetic?' spat Agatha.

Casper was surprised to find he actually felt some sympathy for Bernie.

What did a record matter if it didn't even make you happy?

'Bernie, you've done some truly horrible things,' he started. 'Once we're back on dry land you'll have a lot to answer for . . . But that record. It was really something.'

Bernie looked up, his interest piqued.

'You swam the English Channel,' added Beryl. 'Before your twelfth birthday!'

'That's nothing to be sniffed at,' said Casper.

The hint of a smile betrayed Bernie's emotions

and his ears burnt red, allowing Casper to catch the slightest glimpse of the famous 'Baby Face' for just a fleeting moment.

'But records are made to be broken.'

Bernie stared at the web-toed boy from underneath his wild eyebrows. 'Records are made to be broken,' he repeated, chewing the sentence over in his mind. It was like a fog had finally lifted after years of cloudy misery. Suddenly, Bernie was doubled over laughing.

'Records are made to be broken!' he howled. 'My word, I think you're right.'

Casper laughed, and Wynn slapped him on the back with a smile. 'That's why you need to get back in the water and finish your swim.'

'What?'

'Finish it for us,' said Tan. 'Finish it for all of the kids who've come before you; every one of us who's ever dreamt of doing something special.'

'But I've been disqualified. Even if they ignore the webbed feet, I've left the water and drunk half a cup of tea on board *Les Moules-Frites*!'

'Who cares?' laughed Ida. 'We'll know that you've done it.'

'*You'll* know,' added Beryl, her arm through Ida's.

'An official record won't make you any happier,' said Bernie. 'Take it from someone who knows.'

'You'll never be a legend,' crowed Agatha, standing slowly. Her purple eyes were on Casper, scrutinizing him with the same unyielding stare, but the effect was no longer palpable. 'No one will know your name and you'll have *nothing* to show for it!'

'Yes, he will,' said Ida. She lifted the golden medal from her neck and held the trinket out to Casper. 'I know it's not brand new, but you'll have earnt this and ten more in my opinion.'

Nerves, excitement and gratitude battled inside Casper's stomach, and he went to hug his grandmother.

'No,' said Bernie. 'That isn't Casper's medal—'

'Bernie!' shouted Ida and Beryl, unified in anger.

'When he's finished the crossing he'll be the youngest person to ever swim the Channel,' he continued, taking his own emerald ribbon off and placing it in Casper's open palm. 'This is the medal you deserve.'

'You can't!' shrieked Agatha.

'I have, Mother.'

Casper stared down at the shimmering medal where the merman embossed in the gold winked back from behind his monocle.

Could he still do this?

He turned to the bow of the boat and looked across the open sea, which now rippled gently in the breeze – calmer than anything he'd seen since arriving in Corallium. His webbed toes rippled as the familiar longing ran up through his body and into every limb. The sea called to him, even now, asking that he dive back in, like two old friends meeting up after a lifetime.

'Keep this safe,' he said to Bernie, placing the medal back in the man's bony hand. 'Just until I've earnt it . . .'

'So, are we doing this?' asked Wynn, grinning like a Cheshire cat.

Dev ran back to the helm of the tugboat. 'We've only drifted a few hundred metres. Casper can make up the distance in no time!'

Tan slapped him on the back encouragingly.

'We're all here for you,' his mother said.

'Cheering every stroke!' added Dad.

Suddenly Ida the Delmare Dolphin and Beryl the

Bazooka were at his side: Casper's two heroes, ready to cheer him on the final stretch towards France.

'C'mon, kid,' said Beryl with a wink. 'Get back in that water pronto! We haven't got all day, y'know.'

Ida smiled with tears in her eyes. 'Your drive and passion are a testament to the people of Corallium, and to our family. I'm so proud of you, Casper.'

She pulled her grandson into a tight embrace.

Suddenly, the sides of Casper's neck began to throb. He placed a hand to his throat and felt the flapping sensation of a phantom pair of gills – an echo from another lifetime.

He felt like he could swim the world.

'I'm doing it for you,' said Casper, pulling on his goggles.

He hopped on to the railing of *Les Moules-Frites*, taking one last look at his friends, before flipping backwards and falling into the welcoming waters of the English Channel with an enormous splash.

Arrivée

𝒯he orange light on Casper's swimming cap blinked through the night, ticking in time with every stroke of his arm. He'd been swimming for hours, though he couldn't say how many, watching as the sun set on the western horizon in a blaze of colour. It had stretched across the sky and bathed *Les Moules-Frites* in a fiery glow.

Ahead, the lights of France had been blinking

white and yellow for a short while, like twinkling fireflies growing ever closer. Soon, Casper could see the cliffs of Cap Gris-Nez calling him forward, the moonlight washing its chalky face with an angelic halo of mist. Slowly, dense mats of bright pink began to dot the landscape, the flowering petals of large swathes of sea thrifts illuminated under the stars like celebratory bouquets – awaiting Casper's triumphant landing.

Not long now, he thought, pushing himself forward in spite of the burning in his arms. His goggles were cloudy and his skin white with cold. His webbed feet ached with a dull pulse, but they kicked steadily even now . . .

Ida, Beryl, his parents and his friends continued to cheer loudly beside him, the dark water stretching between his body and the tugboat which bobbed swiftly as the waves began to bend their way into the approaching shore.

'*Allez*, Casper!' called Wynn. '*Tu peux le faire*, you're so close now!'

From the cliffs rose a concrete lighthouse, slate grey and spinning an amber light from its summit. It guided Casper into land, like so many ships which would pass through the cape every day. The beach ahead was littered with mossy rocks and boulders, and the promise of solid ground was too much. Casper felt his arms flood with urgency.

With his face in the water he pushed onward, and the opaque waters gradually began to lighten in colour. Casper realized quickly that the seabed was rising to meet him, inviting his tired feet to rest on its welcoming palm.

Not yet, he thought.

Les Moules-Frites had fallen back, the water too shallow for its hull, but Casper's friends cheered more wildly than ever as the gap continued to grow between them.

The tips of his webbed toes brushed sand and his heart almost exploded from excitement, happiness, relief. He clambered forward, feeling his shoulders leave the water for the first time in hours as he finally placed the soles of his feet on solid ground.

But no time to rest just yet.

Casper ran up the beach to climb the nearest rock, his arms in the air once his body finally cleared the water and his feet left the sea.

He had done it.

A horn sounded from on board *Les Moules-Frites* and rang across the water with his friends' cries of victory. Casper exhaled, exhausted and elated, and his feet rippled with a familiar sensation of longing – his body desperate, once again, to feel the rush of water across his webbed toes.

A Note from the Author

Casper's dream is to swim the English Channel before he turns twelve, making him the youngest person to ever do so. In reality, he would have to wait a while longer for the chance. Since 2000, anyone wishing to make the crossing solo must be at least sixteen years old – though to take part in a team relay, twelve is the minimum age requirement.

Thomas Gregory holds the record today, having swum the Channel in 1988 at the age of eleven years and 330 days – just a month shy of his own twelfth birthday. Unless the current rules were to change, this incredible achievement is unbeatable.

At the time of writing, Otto Thaning is the oldest person to have completed the swim at an equally impressive age of seventy-three. There is no upper age limit.

Acknowledgements

Thank you always to the team at Chicken House, for all their hard work in making my second book as special as the first – chiefly, my wonderful editor Kesia. Good luck on your American adventure! You will be so missed. Thank you to Laura, for getting my books across the finish line; to Jazz, Liv and Elinor for sending them around the world; and to our captain Barry Cunningham for everything. Thanks, too, to Rachel, designer Steve and the wonderful illustrator Maxine Lee-Mackie for creating another *incredible* cover. I can't wait to see my two books side by side on the shelf.

The launch of my debut novel was more exciting and rewarding than I could have imagined. To every single bookseller who has read or recommended *The Peculiar Tale of the Tentacle Boy* – there aren't the words to express my gratitude, nor the importance of what you do for unknown authors. A very special thank you to Waterstones, and the team at Westbourne Bookshop just a stone's throw from my writing spot on the Dorset sands.

To all of the teachers, librarians, parents, bloggers, vloggers and teaching assistants who have supported my work – thank you. There is nothing better than hearing a child has enjoyed my book, or is begging to find out when the next one's coming (I hope they will like Casper's story just as much as Marina's). A special thanks to Scott Evans and Tom Griffiths for being total champions.

An enormous thanks to my marvellous agent Lauren, and the incredible team at Bell Lomax Moreton – especially Paul, Justine and Julie – for their unswerving guidance, input and advice. A drink is in order!

Thank you to each and every one of my brilliant friends for their joy and enthusiasm in sharing the news of my books far and wide – it means the world. To my author pals, thank you for helping make this publishing lark a little bit less of a mystery: Andy, Ben and Sam for their humour and friendship, Jennifer for her kind words, Alexandra, Ayrton, The Good Ship and all my fellow Chickens – namely Efua, Holly and Jasbinder – for promoting such a warm and welcoming coop.

My family have a favourite story from when I

was six, on holiday in Florida. One morning we were off to visit SeaWorld, but I was so happy to be swimming in the hotel pool I flatly refused to leave it. My dad was forced to drag me from the water, where I promptly clung to a lamp post before finally being flung inside the car. I like to think I was aware of the evils of SeaWorld even then, but really, I just *loved* being in the water. Nothing has changed, and, like Casper, you could find me in a river or the sea on any day of the year . . . So thank you to my family for the stories, my dad for Sunday swimming lessons and Andrea for answering my endless questions about the Channel (though I've surely taken some liberties). An enormous thank you to my mum for her incredible support, over the last few years in particular, and to my wonderful boyfriend Rob for being the very best one there is.

This book is dedicated to my two grannies, and if you've read this far you will understand why. But I must also thank my grandad and grandpa, who had an equal part in making childhood summers by the sea so incredibly special. When I wrote the first words of this novel outside our Bournemouth beach hut, I was lucky to still have three grandparents despite being well into my thirties. While they're no longer here to read this finished story, their immense passion for the sea lives on in these pages.